# *A LIFE APART*

P9-APP-217

# A LIFE APART

Shirlee Evans

HERALD PRESS
Scottdale, Pennsylvania
Waterloo, Ontario

**Library of Congress Cataloging-in-Publication Data**
Evans, Shirlee, 1931-
    A life apart / Shirlee Evans.
        p.   cm.
    Summary: Gail's marriage is shaken when the daughter
she gave up for adoption fifteen years ago reenters her life.
Sequel to "A Life In Her Hands."
    ISBN 0-8361-3536-9
    [1. Adoption—Fiction.  2. Mother and child—Fiction.
3. Marriage—Fiction.  4. Christian life—Fiction.]   I. Title.
PS3555.V26L54  1990
813'.54—dc20
[Fic]                                                        90-42762
                                                                 CIP
                                                                  AC

A LIFE APART
Copyright © 1990 by Herald Press, Scottdale, Pa. 15683
    Published simultaneously in Canada by Herald Press,
    Waterloo, Ont. N2L 6H7. All rights reserved.
Library of Congress Catalog Number: 90-42762
International Standard Book Number: 0-8361-3536-9
Printed in the United States of America
Design by Merrill Miller/Cover art by Roger Cooke

1 2 3 4 5 6 7 8 9 10 96 95 94 93 92 91 90

# Contents

*To all who asked:
Whatever became of
Gail and her baby?*

# 1

## Listen to Me!

"What do you mean, it's fine with you?" Gail Lorring demanded as she stood at the kitchen island stove top in her husband's fire-red robe, sleeves rolled to her elbows. In one hand she held a spatula, in the other a pot holder.

Tilting her head to one side, she lifted a shoulder to her cheek to brush back the thick blunt-cut chestnut hair. She flopped a slightly mangled over-easy egg onto a plate beside two limp wedges of pale toast, then stepped around the counter to where Brad stood adjusting his tie.

"I don't *want* my mother living close to us. I don't *want* her influencing our sons, hurting them the way she hurt me while I was growing up. Can't you understand that?"

Brad shook his head as he spun a low-backed bar stool around and sat at the counter. His reddish gold hair was rumpled from running his fingers through it as though trying to strain out his wife's heated words. "No. I don't understand."

Gail slammed the plate down. She glared at the back of his head before sliding the plate in front of him. "That's because you haven't been listening. Like when I tried talking to you the other night. You blew up before I could explain how I felt about Abigail."

"I told you when we met we'd never bring that up again." His tone sharpened. "So you had a baby years ago and gave her up for adoption. So what?"

Gail stared. "So what? When I first told you, you said I should be proud I'd carried my baby to term. Grateful I'd given her to a couple unable to have a baby."

"I didn't say I wanted to hear about it for the rest of my life." He picked up a fork.

"I've rarely mentioned it. At least not until recently. It's been nearly fifteen years since Abigail's birth. She's almost the age I was when I got pregnant."

Brad ate silently.

"Now my mother, who wouldn't stop drinking long enough to help me keep Abigail, decides she wants to be a grandma to our sons. And you can't see why that should upset me. As far as I'm concerned, she's never earned that right."

Continuing to eat slowly, Brad muttered, "She offered to help you keep Abigail. But you didn't give her the chance."

Gail slid onto a stool at the end of the counter, turning to watch him. "You'll argue toenail to toenail with me about other things, like my mother's plans to move here. But as soon as I mention my daughter, you slam the door."

He glanced at her, a half smile on his still-youthful face, then evaded her eyes. "I just sat down to eat. I haven't slammed anything. Yet—"

With a sigh Gail closed her eyes for a moment. "You know what I mean, Brad. You lock me away."

"Let's face it, you've been badgering me about this for days, even though I've told you I don't intend discussing it. There's nothing I can do about Abigail. I didn't know you then. There's no use knocking ourselves out over a girl neither of us knows. You saw her for only a few minutes after she was born.

"Besides," he turned half around, looking toward the door leading to the rest of the house, "I don't think we should go into this now. I thought you didn't want the boys hearing about their half sister yet."

"Then let's go out for dinner this weekend so we *can* talk. I'm sure Jenny would watch the boys." Gail moved to the stool next to him and reached for his hand. "I really do need to talk to you about Abigail."

"Why?" he demanded. "Talk! That's all you women ever want to do." Pushing the nearly empty plate away, he pulled his hand from hers, drained his glass of orange juice, then stood. "I don't want to hear anymore about this." His blue-green eyes bored into Gail's.

Taken off guard by the harshness of his voice, Gail could only stare. She had never seen him this angry. He was usually so calm.

His body lost some rigidity as he glanced away, shaking his head. "I'm sorry. I'm tired from the long hours I've been putting in at the paper. The crime series we've been working on has about sapped me."

Unwilling to deepen his anger, Gail merely nodded. But she thought, *He's using his work as an excuse.* Yes, he had been working longer hours, but she doubted that was why he refused to discuss Abigail.

Looking down at her hands clasped on the counter top, she finally remarked, "I know you've been working hard and you're tired. But won't you please help me find a way to stop my mother from moving here?"

"No. I like your mother. She may be a little frayed around the edges, but there's a lot of heart to the woman."

Pulling a dark suit jacket on over his long slim frame, Brad turned back for a moment. He was having to dress up more since his promotion from reporter to head of the news department. "I think we might be able to get your mom and Tom going to church with us. She's stopped drinking. When we met Tom at their wedding he seemed a pretty decent sort."

"Brad, right now is a bad time for me." Standing up and going to her husband, Gail lifted her arms to encircle his neck.

"I wish you'd try to understand my feelings. My mother moving here only adds to the hurt of that time fifteen years ago. Even though you refuse to talk about it, the fact remains my daughter will soon be the same age I was when I gave her up. Can't you see what that's doing to me?"

He stiffened and pulled back from her. "I see what it's doing to *us*! You're not some wide-eyed kid anymore. You claim to believe in God. Why can't you just leave it in God's hands? Let go of the thing! You're like a dog constantly gnawing and chewing away at a bone."

Glancing at his watch he turned toward the back door. "Hey, I've got to run. I mean, literally. I have an appointment in ten minutes."

Gail lifted a hand to wave as she stood in the doorway, but he didn't look back. With a sigh she closed the door. It was time to wake the boys for school.

As usual, Jimmy woke smiling, ready for another day at kindergarten. He was so like his father, freckles, reddish hair and all. Jimmy had been exuberant over his first day of class just weeks before. Puffing his chest, he had declared, "I'm big and 'portant now, too. Just like Grant!"

Seven-year-old Grant, with brown eyes, darker hair, and a serious oval face like his mother's, was in no hurry for another day of second grade. His friends at school had tempered his enthusiasm. By the time you reached second grade, it wasn't cool to admit you liked school.

Gail phoned Jenny as soon as she had the boys on the school bus. "Can I come over? I've *got* to talk to someone. Since you already know nearly all there is to know about me, you're the only one I *can* talk to."

"Sure," Jenny agreed.

Later, over a second cup of coffee on Jenny's glassed-in sun porch, Gail spilled out the morning scene as they watched leaves fall from the old oak tree in the backyard. Although the breeze was chilly, the sky remained clear.

"Am I just whining?" Gail asked as she finished.

"Well—" Jenny smiled, dimples puncturing a pert face framed by short dark curls. "It's something you might want to guard against."

Brought up short, Gail stared at the petite young woman. Jenny was probably the best friend she'd ever had. Gail smiled. "Good old Jen. I can always count on you to tell it like you see it."

"That's what friends are for. At least good friends— which is what we are."

Gail nodded. "The best."

Jenny reached for a cookie from the plate she had placed on a plant stand between them. "So what do you plan to do about your mother moving here with her new husband? Have you looked at apartments for them yet, like she asked you to?"

"I've glanced through the classifieds."

A mischievous spark danced in Jenny's eyes. "You know, if you leave it up to your mom, she might find a place next door to you. Don't you think you'd better get busy?"

"I have to work the rest of the week. That was another thing I wanted to talk about. Can you keep the boys an extra day and a half?"

"Sure. But I thought you were supposed to work only two and a half days a week."

"The woman I job-share with is sick. They asked me to cover for her. I could look at apartments for Mom and Tom in the evening, though. Brad's going to be working late for awhile."

Then changing the subject, Gail remarked thoughtfully, "Remember I told you how great Brad was when I first told him about the baby I gave up for adoption? Before I was a Christian?"

Jenny nodded. "When you two met at camp?"

"Yes. At the church camp I volunteered for every summer after my daughter was born. I was nineteen when I met Brad. He was a year older. I told him about Abigail one evening when we stayed behind at the camp fire after the kids had been herded off to bed.

"He was so understanding, assuring me I'd made a wise choice in having my baby and giving it up for adoption. Afterward he said we'd never need talk about it again. That was fine with me—at the time. But I see now his never *meant* never."

Gail took another sip of coffee, letting her mind wander back to her wedding eight years before. Moving with Brad to Linden had meant leaving the insurance company where she had worked since leaving high school.

Four years before that, after her baby's birth at a Salvation Army home, Gail had returned to live with her foster family until she finished high school. Steve's father, grandfather of the baby, then financed a three-month computer class for her.

Soon after she went to work she had rented a small studio apartment. A warm feeling coursed over Gail as she recalled remaining close to Sue and Mack Grant, her Christian foster parents, who had helped her find new meaning through faith in Jesus. She had named Brad's and her first son after the Grants.

At the time of her marriage to Brad he had just finished college, and had been accepted for his first job as a reporter on the Linden Globe. She vividly recalled leaving the town where she had been born and raised to move the 150 miles to Linden with him.

"Where are you, Gail?" Jenny was singsonging. "I was asking about your mother."

"I was just remembering. You know, Jen, when my mother came to our wedding she was drunk! Can you believe that? She carried on and on at the reception about how she hadn't had anything to do with the wedding plans."

"She probably felt left out," Jenny offered.

"Sue asked her to help. Invited her to go over the plans with us. But Mom never showed up."

Jenny drew in a resigned breath. "Alcoholics are unpredictable when under the influence."

"I know. And I'm thankful she's stopped drinking. This man she married seems good for her. He's quiet. Several years older than Mom. They seemed happy when we went to their wedding a few months ago."

Leaning closer Jenny hesitantly suggested, "It might be good having your mom close. Brad could be right about getting them started to church with you."

Gail shrugged. "Maybe—"

"Don't go off the deep end about this. We're to honor our parents. You have only your mother since you don't know who your father is."

"Neither does my mother!" Gail added bitterly.

Jenny nodded. "It seems to me you may soon have to forgive this woman who gave you birth twenty-nine years ago."

The two sat in silence for several minutes, the only sound a falling acorn bouncing off the roof. Finally Gail stood up to stare out at the carpet of fallen leaves.

Jenny shifted uncomfortably. "I'm sorry, Gail. I have no right telling you what to do. How you should feel. I just hate seeing you so consumed."

"I'm mixed up, Jen. I know you're right. But how can I stop blaming my mother for stealing my childhood?"

Getting to her feet, Jenny put her arms around Gail. "I don't know. I'd probably have as hard a time as you in your place. Gail, pray about it. Let the Lord help. With God all things *are* possible."

After Gail and the boys had eaten dinner alone that evening, Gail took them across town to look at apartments listed in the paper.

"It'll be fun having Grandma live here," Grant said from the front seat.

"Yeah," Jimmy piped from the back. "My friend at school says grandmas' buy stuff for kids."

"I wouldn't set your hopes too high," Gail told them. "You can never be sure what your grandmother will or won't do."

"How come you don't like her, Mom?" Grant asked. "She *is* your mother. And she makes us laugh."

Gail clenched her fingers tighter around the steering wheel. "It's not that I don't like her. It's just that—Well, let's just say she wasn't always a good mother while I was growing up. I've told you how I had to live with other families before I was old enough to be on my own."

"That was when you stayed with the Grants," their namesake announced knowingly.

Gail nodded. "They were the last family I lived with. They were more like my parents than my own mom."

She pulled up in front of the first apartment building and scooted the boys out of the car. They trailed her into the first building, then into another and another. Later they stopped at a bakery for a bag of cinnamon donuts before heading home.

Once there Gail called her mother. "I've found three pretty nice apartments."

"Well, thanks Gail. I was wondering if we were going to hear from you. We've given notice here and have to be out by the end of the month. I told Tom if you didn't find us something soon, we'd have to move in with you and Brad until we did find a place."

Although amusement shaded Beverly's voice, Gail had a feeling she might have meant it.

When Brad came home the boys were asleep. Gail was in the kitchen ironing a skirt to wear to work. Brad slapped a stack of papers on the counter.

"You look tired," she said.

He shook his head. "I'm beyond tired. I'm exhausted. You can't believe what goes on behind the scenes. Even in a town the size of Linden."

"You're talking about that crime series?"

He nodded. "What's to eat? I had dinner downtown, but I'm hungry again."

"I stopped at a bakery this evening when I went to look at apartments for my mother. There are donuts in the bag on the counter."

He poured a glass of milk and took a donut, sitting down to watch her. "So you finally looked for a place. Find anything interesting?"

"Three. I called and told her. They're driving up to-morrow to look. They've given notice where they live and have to be out by the end of the month."

"Did you invite them to stay the night?"

"No." She glared at him across the ironing board. "I have to work the rest of the week. Remember?"

"Still, honey, that's a long drive back after looking at apartments all afternoon. The boys will be disap-pointed if they don't get to see them. Whether you like it or not, your mom wowed the kids when we went to her wedding."

Setting the iron on its heel, Gail slapped both hands flat on the board top. "I don't want to buddy up to her so soon. What if instead of us introducing Mom to the Lord, she twists Grant and Jimmy around to her way of thinking? To her lifestyle?"

Brad returned her gaze, not replying at once. Final-ly he said hesitantly, "I doubt there's much danger of that. She's not such a bad person since she stopped drinking. We'll always have more influence on our sons than your mother."

Unplugging the iron, Gail placed it beside the stove top to cool. "But there *is* that possibility."

# 2

## Outmaneuvered

As Gail slid onto a stool beside her husband he cautiously leaned toward her. "Are we still mad?"

She reached for a donut. "I'm too tired."

"Good!" Brad heaved an exaggerated sigh. "I was dreading coming home." He stared into her dark eyes. "Has the fight been called off, or are we between rounds?"

"You're making it sound worse than it was. It's just that when you won't let me talk to you about what's bothering me it seems you don't care. Maybe we need counseling or something."

"Where do you get that 'we' stuff!"

Gail drew a deep breath. "Brad, I can't simply turn off thinking about Abigail. Especially now. I keep wondering if she might be going through the same things I did at her age. I wonder what she's like. Is she happy? Does she have a boy friend? Does she wonder about me? Will she—"

"Whoa, Gail!" Brad interrupted. "You've got to try to let her go. I love you. You have two boys who love you and need you. Your faith in God can help you deal with the pain you're feeling."

"And I have a daughter lost to me forever." Gail glanced away as tears filled her eyes.

Brad jumped to his feet, his expression hardening. "There are worse things. A lot worse! You're beginning to sound like a spoiled brat."

Gail flinched. "I'm not like that, honey. It's just that—" But Brad had stalked from the room, leaving her and the donuts behind. She sighed and pulled another from the bag. She took a bite then laid it aside. She was tired. He was tired. She had picked a bad time to press him again.

Could Brad be jealous of Steve, the boy who had fathered her first child? she wondered. She regretted that intimacy. Brad had been raised in a Christian home and had no doubt come chaste to their marriage bed.

What he had just told her was right. She had so much to be thankful for. She loved Brad and their sons. Their marriage had been good. Other women complained their husbands wouldn't talk to them about important things. But Brad had always been open, and sensitive to her feelings and moods. It was only when her first pregnancy came up that he withdrew.

Up to now it hadn't been much of a problem. But as Abigail Marie (the name she and the baby's adoptive parents had chosen together) neared fifteen, the old hurts and memories refused to depart.

The next morning Brad left without breakfast, informing her he would eat downtown. There was no time to brood over it. She had the boys to get off to school. There were notes to write so they could ride the bus back to Jenny's where they'd stay until she picked them up after work.

"Aren't we ever gonna see Dad again?" Jimmy complained as she drove them to Jenny's house.

Gail had decided to go to the office early to make up for the time she'd take off when her mother and Tom stopped by. The boys would catch the bus with Jenny's daughter Kim.

"Yeah," Grant noted from the backseat (it was his turn to ride there), "Now I know how Mark feels. He's had to live with just his mom since his dad went away."

"Thanks a lot!" Gail sputtered, pretending to be hurt. "You make it sound as though living with just your mother is only a notch below being shipped off to Siberia."

Jimmy looked at her inquiringly. "What's a Si—Si-ber-a?"

"It's not a what. It's a where. A place in Russia that's real cold."

"We never see Dad anymore," Grant complained.

"You saw him last weekend."

Feeling left out, Jimmy piped up, "I don't even remember what he looks like."

"Oh, come on now!" He giggled as Gail tousled his hair.

After hurried kisses good-bye at Jenny's house, Gail drove downtown to the three-story office building where she had worked for the last two months. When Jimmy reached kindergarten age this fall she had found a time-share position with the same firm that had employed her before moving to Linden. It had worked well until Linda, the woman who shared the job, got sick. Actually, Gail thought as she parked her car, she really didn't mind. It was better than moping around the house in her present state of mind.

She told the receptionist her mother would be coming to see her later, rode the elevator to the third floor, and tried to lose herself behind her computer monitor. As she processed claims in the large open room shared by ten other employees, her eyes kept wandering to the big hexagon shaped clock on the wall. How long would it take her mother and Tom to reach Linden?

It was eleven-thirty when Gail was finally called to the lobby. As she walked to the elevator, another such time flashed in memory. She had been called to the visitors lounge while at the Salvation Army Home awaiting Abigail's birth. There she found her mother. Beverly had come to invite Gail to return home with her baby. But Gail refused, positive it wouldn't work as long as her mother kept drinking and bringing men to the house.

The elevator door slid open, bringing Gail back to the present. She stepped out to greet Beverly and the tall, gray-haired man her mother had so recently married.

Beverly sat in the corner beside a potted fig, her eyes fixed on the elevator. She smiled when she saw Gail. The former Beverly Richards was still slim and attractive in her late fifties. Gail wished she could feel something other than she did for this woman who had given her birth while still married to the man Gail once thought of as her father. The man who had left them after discovering Gail was not his child.

Streaks of gray ran through the shoulder-length tresses of Beverly's once harsh black hair. Gail wished she could forget the day she first learned about her parentage—the day she told her mother she herself was pregnant.

Tom Duncan, Gail's stepfather, was looking out the window. He turned as Gail approached, smiling warmly. She recalled the image she used to conjure up of a father she would never—could never—know. Realizing she would never know him had helped her release her own child to a couple she knew only as Jim and Kathy.

"Gail!" Beverly stood, planting a kiss on her daughter's cheek.

Gail pulled back involuntarily. At least it was good not to smell liquor.

"I didn't know if they'd mind us bothering you at work or not. But you did tell us to stop by."

"It's okay."

The woman looked around. "It's a nice building. I'm so proud of you having a job like this. It shouldn't be near as hard as waitressing like I used to do. But then I didn't have anyone like Steve's father to finance training for me. Could we see your office?"

Growing uncomfortable, Gail responded, "I don't really have an office. It's just a large room with a lot of desks."

As she turned to Tom, Gail made an effort to smile. "How long did it take to get here?"

"About an hour and a half. It was a nice drive with the leaves changing color. Although your mother," he stepped close to Beverly, putting his arm around her, "was much too anxious to see you and the boys to enjoy the scenery."

"I'm sorry you won't be able to see them," Gail said, realizing they must have planned to come to the house later. "Brad's working late at the office every evening now. The boys go to a friend's house after school until I get off work."

Disappointment shaded Beverly's face. "Oh—" Then

she brightened. "We could see the boys for a few minutes before driving back home. You could give us directions to your friend's house."

Gail started to shake her head. But she was saved by Tom, who noted, "I don't believe we'll have time this trip, dear. Besides, it won't be long until we'll be living here. You'll have plenty of time to spend with your grandsons then."

Gail wished she could think of a painless way to let her mother know she didn't want her to get chummy with her grandsons. Instead she changed the subject.

She handed Tom the addresses of the apartments she had seen the night before, the classified section of the newspaper, and a map of the city. Then she glanced at her watch. "I've got to get back to work. I marked the apartments I looked at on the map. You shouldn't have any trouble finding them."

As Gail turned toward the elevator, Beverly called her back, reaching a hand to her daughter. "Is this a problem for you? Us living so close? Please don't let us move here, then refuse me time with you and your family."

Her mother's longing tugged at Gail's conscience. Turning to God had made her want to feel different about her mother. But how could she *not* feel as she did? She hedged. "We don't have much extra time with both of us working."

"Maybe after we move I can take care of the boys. While you're at work," Beverly offered, glancing at her husband. "Tom loves children."

"They like staying with Jenny. She has an eight-year-old girl they play with after school."

Taking his wife's arm, Tom guided Beverly toward the door. "There'll be time to talk later."

"But, Tom. If I can't see my daughter and her children, then—"

Pushing her fears from her, Gail interrupted, "You'll see a lot of us, Mom. I promise."

The month dragged on for a depressed Gail. The more she tried to escape thoughts of Abigail, the more miserable she became. And the more she tried forcing herself to see the positive side of her mother's move, the more she dreaded it.

The crime series Brad had been working on was finally published. Gail expected him to be home more after that. But he wasn't. Now a new worry assaulted her. Had she driven Brad to another woman? It was difficult to believe such a thing of her husband. Yet he *had* changed. Their relationship was definitely strained.

Her mother and Tom's moving day arrived on a cold damp Saturday as bits of icy snow peppered the wind-driven rain. *A good day*, Gail thought as she rose from her warm bed to look out the window, *for a book and a fire in the fireplace after the house was cleaned.*

As usual, Gail put on the red robe she had given Brad for Christmas three years before. Brad was cooking breakfast when she sleepily entered the kitchen.

"I called Tom awhile ago," he said. "I told him we'd drive down to help them pack. I invited them to stay with us until they get things arranged in their new place."

"You could have asked me first," Gail suggested warily.

"You would have tried to stop me, and I fully intended on doing it anyway."

She sat at the counter as he mixed his favorite pancake batter peppered with fresh apple chunks. "Why do you keep trying to throw me and Mom together when you know how it hurts?"

Brad shrugged. "It wasn't my idea they move here. But once they made up their minds, I felt one of us should make them feel welcome."

"Yet you don't seem to care how I feel."

"Your mother did wrong. But you're overlooking one strong point in her favor."

"And that is?"

"She carried you to term, even though she took a chance of breaking up her marriage. Which is what happened."

"What's so great about that? She had no choice. Abortion wasn't legal then."

"Oh, come on, Gail. A streetwise gal like your mom? Of course she had a choice. She could have found a way. But she didn't."

Gail sat staring at him as he headed toward the living room. "You think about it while I get the boys up. But if you're going with us, you'd better get dressed."

With a sigh, Gail went back to the bedroom, pulling on jeans and a lavender sweatshirt.

Grant and Jimmy were wild to go help Grandma— and Grandpa, as they were already calling Tom. Brad was unusually cheerful as they drove back to the town where Gail had been born.

Gail thought about Brad's praise of her mom. Beverly had once admitted she'd held the breakup of her marriage against Gail for a time. How would Brad excuse that? She would have pushed the point if the boys hadn't been with them.

When they reached her mother and Tom's apartment, Gail threw herself into packing boxes and carrying them to the U-Haul truck Tom had rented. She had been concerned the boys might get underfoot. But her mother handled them surprisingly well, giving each small duties, making them feel a part of what was going on. It was a side of her mother she had never seen.

Later in the afternoon Gail dialed the Grant's number, asking Sue if she could drop in for a few minutes before leaving town. It had been some time since Gail had seen her foster parents. Beverly looked hurt, although she said nothing.

Jimmy begged to go along, but Gail told him, "No. Not this time. You stay here with Daddy."

"And Grandma," Jimmy responded, hugging the woman Gail had longed as a child to be hugged by.

Sue came out of the house as Gail drove into the Grants' driveway a few minutes later. While Sue's fawn-colored hair was graying, her smile remained warm and infectious. She spoke not a word when Gail reached her, enveloping her foster daughter in her arms.

There were tears in Sue's eyes when they pulled apart. "I nearly called you last night to see if we could get together. I've been thinking about you so much lately."

"And about Abigail?"

Nodding, Sue pulled her into the house. "Yes. She'll soon be fifteen."

"You've kept track then," Gail noted with satisfaction. "I guess you're just about the only one, besides myself, who cares or understands how I feel right now."

"Well Gail!" Mack's voice boomed as he walked into the living room. "Hey, kid. You're looking great."

She blushed. Mack always made her do that. "Thanks."

After he left the room Gail poured out her hurts to the woman who had been like a mother to her.

"Brad won't allow you to talk about this?" Sue asked.

"He either refuses, leaves the house, or gets mad."

"It sounds like he's fighting some kind of emotional battle. He was a Christian when you two met. He came from a home with values different than yours. It may bother him to be continually reminded another man fathered your firstborn."

"I suppose," Gail said hesitantly. "But Brad's really not like that. He's so open about most things. He's been such a caring, understanding person until lately.

"I still feel good about the decision I made regarding Abigail. It's just that right now, as she reaches the age I was when she was born, I can't help wondering . . . I mean—"

"You're afraid she might make the same mistakes you made?"

Gail nodded. "Yes. If she did, she'd be the third generation to do so."

"Are you sure you don't have something else in mind, Gail? Are you maybe wanting to locate her? To see her?"

"No. Although I *would* like to know where she is and what's going on in her life. If I could just talk to Kathy, the woman who adopted her, I think I'd be satisfied."

Sighing, Gail glanced around the room as Ginger's photo caught her eye on the mantel. "How is Ginger? Have she and her husband made you a grandmother yet?"

"No. Not yet. They live in the West Coast. Ginger's still teaching junior high."

Looking down at her hands in her lap, Gail rubbed one thumb over the back of the other. "And Steve? Have you heard anything about him?"

"I saw his mother the other day. He's a doctor now.

He and his wife live on the East Coast."

"Last time I talked to him was when he visited me at the hospital before Abigail was born. It was such a shock to learn he was hurting too over our baby. I didn't think he cared."

"I understand his wife recently gave birth to a little girl."

"So Steve has a daughter. Do you suppose he ever thinks of Abigail? Of his first daughter?"

# 3

## *Unreasoning Anger*

It was late by the time Tom and Beverly's things were unloaded at their new apartment in Linden. They were all tired. Overflowing boxes were stacked in the middle of the floor and against the walls when Brad threw up his hands, shoved one last bulging carton into a corner, and declared the day over.

"Come on. Let's go out to dinner. My treat. Enough's enough!"

After eating at a nearby smorgasbord, Beverly and Tom went home with Brad and Gail to spend the night in their spare bedroom. As soon as the boys were bathed and herded off to bed, Gail secluded herself in her own bathroom in a hot tub of bubbles. When she emerged her mother had gone to bed. Tom and Brad were watching the last of a football game Brad had recorded on their VCR that afternoon.

Tom reached out to catch Gail's wrist as she passed. "Thanks for all you did for us today. For your mother, especially. It meant a lot to her."

Pulling gently away, Gail glanced at Brad. "It was Brad—I mean, you're welcome."

She mumbled a good night, then escaped to her room. Gail turned off the light and lay there feeling her heart pound. This was the first night she had spent under the same roof with her mother since she was twelve—seventeen years ago.

Vividly she recalled the day she had been taken from her mother. By then Beverly was drinking nearly every waking hour. One foster home after another followed until Gail ended up at the Grants, met Steve, and become pregnant. From the Grants she was sent to the Salvation Army home to have her baby. Then she lived again with Sue, Mack, and their daughter Ginger until she graduated from high school and could support herself.

She thought of Steve as she stared at the shadowy ceiling. So he and his wife had a daughter. She was happy for him. She was happy for herself, too. She loved Brad. Her fear that he had found someone else was no doubt groundless. Although Brad might well find someone else if she didn't get a grip on herself.

The next morning at breakfast Brad thanked the Lord for the food, then turned to his mother-in-law. "Why don't you and Tom come to church with us this morning?"

"Oh, we couldn't. There's too much to do at the apartment." Beverly shook her head. "Some other time maybe."

"I'll come by later to help you put things away," Gail heard herself offering.

Brad smiled at his wife, then turned to Tom. "We'll both be over after church."

Monday found Gail weary from their busy weekend.

She was glad she didn't have to go to work until Wednesday afternoon. Linda's shift began Monday and continued through the first half of Wednesday. Gail then took over at noon to finish the week. Resolving to soften her attitude toward her mother, Gail spent Monday morning searching her Bible for the strength and direction she desperately needed.

When she picked up the boys at Jenny's on Thursday after work, Jenny asked, "How's it going with you and your mother?"

"We went to see them last night. They seem okay. She still wants me to leave the boys with her while I work. I may let her take care of them now and then, but not all the time."

"How are things with you and Brad?"

Gail glanced at the boys waiting by the door.

Jenny took the hint. "You know, boys, I'll bet your mom wouldn't mind if you took home some of those cookies I baked this afternoon. Kim, take them out to the kitchen. See if you can find paper bags for their cookies."

Jimmy scrambled for the kitchen with Kim as Grant lagged behind. He glared at his mother as he walked in front of her.

After they left Jenny asked, "Have you heard about the Crisis Pregnancy Center opening here in town? I thought it might help you, as well as the girls, if you got involved." She slipped a pamphlet from her pocket, handing it to Gail. "Here, you can read about it."

Gail hastily stuffed the material into her purse as the boys trailed Kim back to the living room.

"See what we got!" Jimmy announced, joyfully shaking his cookie bag.

"Don't break them," his mother cautioned, glancing at Grant who avoided her eyes. Rising, she herded them toward the door again. "Thanks for everything, Jen. For the cookies, and for this." She patted her purse.

On the drive home Jimmy prattled from one subject to another until Gail lost track. She nodded and offered "uh-huh's" at proper intervals. Grant, on the other hand, remained quiet, barely responding when asked about his day.

Once home, Gail hurriedly started dinner. Brad had been coming home earlier since she had stopped pestering him about Abigail.

She was scrubbing potatoes at the sink when Grant wandered into the kitchen. "Are you all right?" Gail questioned. "You're awfully quiet."

"I guess so," he replied listlessly.

"Did something go wrong at school?"

The boy shook his head, leaning dejectedly against the cabinet, tracing the floor pattern with a toe.

"Something's wrong. I can see that. Won't you tell me?"

He shrugged.

"I might be able to help," his mother offered.

"It's just—" He looked up, his dark eyes moist.

She dropped the potato in the sink, dried her hands, and knelt to brush the hair back from his forehead.

"I don't know what's wrong with everybody," he complained, a fat tear splashing on the floor. Wiping his nose on the back of a hand, Grant pouted, "Somethin' bad's happening, isn't it?"

Gail pulled him into her arms. "Honey, I don't know what you're talking about."

"I don't neither," he sobbed against the curve of her neck, dampening her blouse. "But every time Jimmy and me come around, you stop talking. Or else you send us away so we can't hear. Like at Jenny's house. You and Dad been doin' it too. Now you're doin' it with Jenny."

"Oh, honey—" She reached for a tissue. "It's just grown-up talk. It's nothing bad."

He finally stopped crying, though he didn't appear convinced.

"Listen, just as soon as Dad comes home and dinner's over, I'll read to you and Jimmy like we used to in the evenings. Okay?"

He nodded, brightening. "Promise?"

"Promise."

"I'll go find the book I want."

Much later, dinner over, the kitchen cleaned, the boys read to and in bed, Gail finally looked at the pamphlet Jenny had given her. Brad was making notes on a pad as he went over the competition's newspapers spread around the living room. She settled herself in a chair across the room to read through the pamphlet before slipping it out of sight under a stack of magazines.

It was good spending a quiet evening with Brad again. Good having him home. How, she wondered, could she have suspected him of being unfaithful? Yes, it happened. Even in Christian families. But not with her Brad!

"How are things at work?" she questioned, longing only to hear his voice.

"Good." He looked up and grinned. "Real good. How about you?"

"I like working. But I'm glad it's only part time for the boys' sakes. Grant was upset earlier, wondering why everybody seemed to be having secrets. I think he realizes we've been arguing."

"Oh?" Brad was giving her his full attention now. "Did you talk him out of it?"

"I tried."

"Have you talked to your mother lately?"

"I've called her a couple of times. She invited us for dinner tomorrow night."

"What did you tell her?"

"That I'd have to talk to you first but thought we could make it."

That wide grin she loved, and had seen so seldom lately, spread across Brad's face. "Good! I'm proud of you!" He pushed the papers aside and patted the sofa, hugging her tight when she went to sit with him. "You're feeling better about things, aren't you? I know I am."

Friday evening's dinner went well. Gail had never seen her mother so domestic. She was obviously enjoying her new role as homemaker. Gail couldn't help but recall the meals Beverly tried putting together when she was a youngster and her mother was drinking.

Before leaving Brad again invited them to church on Sunday. Although Tom made an excuse, he nevertheless promised, "We will. One of these days."

They were standing at the door together when Jimmy grabbed his grandmother's hand, staring into her face. "Me and Grant are gonna be in the Christmas program at our church. Wanna come see us?"

Beverly bent to hug the boy. "I'd like that. You just tell us when and we'll be there."

Thoughts of the Crisis Pregnancy Center kept nudging at Gail all weekend. Finally on Monday she did something about it. Since there was no school due to a teacher preparation day, Gail called her mother to ask if she could leave the boys with her and Tom for a couple of hours while she went after groceries. But it was not only grocery shopping Gail had in mind.

She dropped Grant and Jimmy off, then drove downtown and parked on a side street near Main. Gail hesitated outside what had until recently been a vacant store building. The door had been newly lettered: *Crisis Pregnancy Center*. She turned the knob.

A woman came from the back to meet her. Another woman was sorting boxes of clothing behind a partial partition. Three chairs and a desk occupied the space in front.

"Hello there!" exclaimed a smiling young woman.

"Mrs. Philips?"

"No. She's not here. Is there something I can do for you?"

"I talked to her earlier. She suggested I come down this morning. Will she be back soon? I left my boys with their grandmother and can't be gone long."

"Mrs. Philips is next door at the coffee shop. She wouldn't mind if you went over to see her. Look for a heavyset woman with blond hair."

As Gail entered the coffee shop she spotted a woman she guessed to be in her late forties who fit the description. Her short blond hair was brushed smoothly back from her face. The woman looked up as Gail stopped beside her.

"Are you Mrs. Philips?"

"Yes. May I do something for you?"

"I'm Gail Lorring. I called earlier."

"Oh yes." She motioned to the bench across from her as a waitress stopped by.

Gail ordered a soft drink.

The Philips woman eyed her curiously. "You're not —I'm sorry. I don't mean to jump to conclusions."

"No, I'm not pregnant." Gail laughed, then turned serious. "But I have been. I was fifteen when I gave my baby up for adoption. I've married since then. My husband and I have two sons. But lately I find myself thinking more and more about the daughter I gave up. She'll soon be fifteen, the same age I was when she was born."

The woman reached across the table to touch Gail's hand. "It's something that never leaves us. My older sister went through the same trauma when she was sixteen."

"Then you *do* know."

"I do. I was fourteen. My sister and I were close. I hurt with her and my parents."

"I thought maybe if I volunteered at your Crisis Pregnancy Center—you know, helped out in some way —it might ease the jumbled feelings I'm having right now. But I wanted you to know my background so you'd understand where I was coming from. I mean, in case a girl came along who wanted to talk to someone who had been through it."

"We do need people to help us. But before you could be a counselor you'd have to complete a training program. We're planning to develop a kind of buddy system for girls who come to us, though. You might work into something like that. In the meantime we're getting in boxes of clothing that have to be sorted and washed."

The woman described other services, including a Bible study for women who had already had an abortion and were pregnant again. "I worked at a center like this in another state before coming here. Seventy percent of our clients were still trying to deal with previous abortions, vowing to keep their babies this time. It was as though the second baby could somehow make up for the one they had aborted.

"We'll soon be starting a twenty-four-hour hot line. Volunteers will answer phones from their own homes whenever our office is closed. If you wanted to get involved with that we could get you into the training program."

"It sounds interesting. I could be home with my family and still help."

"Then of course there's always the donated clothing and baby furniture to get ready to give to women and girls who plan to keep their babies."

"I noticed a couple women sorting through things when I stopped in next door."

Mrs. Philips nodded. "A number of our volunteers take the clothing home to wash and iron."

"Do most girls who come to centers like this keep their babies?"

"Yes. We refer those wanting to give up their babies to appropriate adoption agencies. That's another area where we'll be needing help. Some girls have nowhere to go. We want to find families they can stay with until their babies are born. That might be a good way for you and your husband to help."

"I don't believe my husband is going to want to be involved. I think I'd like to give the hot line a try, though."

By the time Gail arrived back at her mother's apartment, the trunk of her car was stuffed with bags of groceries and used clothing from the Center. When Brad walked in the back door later that evening, he found the washing machine swishing the last load back and forth in the laundry room.

"What's all this?" He stared at a stack of folded baby things stacked on the counter.

The boys came bursting into the room. "It's stuff for ladies and their babies," Jimmy announced, passing on the explanation his mother had given.

Grant smiled. "Yeah. I thought she was startin' a store!"

"What's going on?" Brad demanded.

Gail told him of her visit to the Crisis Pregnancy Center without trying to keep anything from the boys. Excitedly she explained what the Center was trying to do.

Her bubble burst when Brad stalked from the room without a word.

"What's wrong with Dad?" Grant questioned, turning to his mother. "Are you and him gonna fight again?"

Gail shook her head. "I baked a chocolate cake for dessert with gooey thick frosting. That ought to put a smile back on your father's face."

It didn't. Dinner was solemn as Gail vainly tried to lift the evening's mood. Finally the boys went to bed.

The minute she came from their room Brad took her by the arm and led her to the garage. "I don't want them to hear us. Especially after you told me how upset Grant was the other day."

Gail tried to pull free, but his fingers bit tighter. "What's wrong with you, Brad?"

"I'd like to know what's wrong with you? Why did you go to that place behind my back?"

"You mean to the Crisis Pregnancy Center?"

"You know that's what I mean. Why?"

"I imagine you know the reason," she said, finally jerking free of him. "I thought it might help. Not only them, but me." She glanced at her arm, where the imprint of his fingers remained.

His face flushed. "I'm sorry. It's just that—"

"Just what?" Gail threw back at him, her eyes ablaze as he stopped in mid sentence. "What on earth is going on with you, Brad? Lots of people—lots of churches—are helping the Center. Why shouldn't I? I'd like to see our own church get involved."

He stood there staring at her. "If I said I'd rather you didn't, would you give it up?"

"No!" she shot back, lifting her chin.

Brad suddenly drew his hand back as though to strike. Quickly she stepped back. "What's wrong with you!"

Gail detected Brad's temper cooling. She waited a moment, then went to him and touched his cheek. "You've always been such a caring person. It was you who jumped in to help Mom and Tom move here. You made them feel welcome while I held back. So why are you so angry that I want to help someone? Is it because the Center reminds you I had a baby before we married?"

When he still didn't respond, she added, "By the way, it should please you to know I left the boys with Mom for awhile this morning. I'm feeling better about her and Tom living here. Mom's changed." Gail stopped when she realized even this wasn't getting through.

Returning to the problem at hand she noted, "I'd really like to help out at the Center, honey. Please don't stand in my way." She smiled, moving closer to encircle his neck with her arms. "I believe it will help me. Won't you tell me why you're so against it?"

He pulled back, eyes cold. "Oh, go ahead. Do whatever you like. You will anyway."

He stomped back into the house, leaving her alone and puzzled. A chill permeated the house as she followed him inside. A short while later Brad announced he had to run back to the office for something. After he left Gail made sure the boys were asleep, then went to the kitchen to call Jenny.

She cried as she told her friend what had happened. "What do you suppose could be wrong with

Brad?" she questioned helplessly.

"I really don't know, Gail. Would you like me to ask Larry to talk to him?"

"No! Please don't. If Brad found out I'd talked to you—Well, I don't know what he'd do. Especially the mood he's in now. Do you think I should forget about volunteering at the Center?"

Jenny hesitated. "I don't like offering advice when I don't know both sides. But I think if I were you I'd tell him I was going to continue unless he gave me a good reason why I shouldn't."

"That's what I was thinking," Gail said. "But what about the Bible statement about the husband being the family leader? Would it be right to go against his wishes?"

"That's a tough one," Jenny admitted. "But the Bible also says husbands are to love their wives, take their needs seriously. Maybe you should give Brad a little more time. Let him cool off, then ask again. Tell him you'll consider not working at the Center—*if* you can come to a mutual agreement why you shouldn't."

# 4

## God-acquitted, Self-accused

Gail packed up the baby clothes and took them out to her car while Brad was gone. She decided she had better get them out of his sight. She would return them to the Center in the morning after the boys left for school.

It was nearly midnight when Brad returned. She was stretched out on the couch, pretending to read, when he walked in the front door and headed straight for their bedroom.

She had come to another decision while Brad was gone. It was time to see Pastor Martin. She had never mentioned her first child to their minister. He had been at the church less than a year and there had been no reason to counsel with him up to then. Now it was time.

As soon as the school bus left next morning, Gail made an appointment with Pastor Martin. Then she drove to the Center.

Mrs. Philips smiled when Gail staggered in with the box of clothing. The smile disappeared when she saw Gail's face. "Is something wrong?"

"My husband, for some strange reason, is dead set against my working with you. I'm on my way now to talk to our pastor."

"If it causes a problem, Gail, it's not worth it. We need volunteers, and I'd really like to have you work with us, but not if it means a house divided."

"I know. I'll try to get things straightened out."

She pulled into the church parking lot ten minutes later. It wouldn't be easy telling her pastor about Abigail. She should have come months ago, when her daughter's approaching birthday began to haunt her.

Mary, Pastor Martin's secretary, greeted her. "Hi, Gail. Go on in. Pastor's expecting you."

The man seated behind the desk rose. "Come in, Gail. You sounded upset over the phone."

She sat on the edge of the offered chair, hesitantly sharing her past with the tall, balding man before bringing him up to date. She hadn't expected her minister to be shocked at learning she had given a baby up for adoption, and he didn't disappoint her. It was getting to be an old story. Even in Christian families.

She told him then of Brad's reaction to her volunteering at the Crisis Pregnancy Center. "Do you think I'm wrong?" she asked.

"I think," he told her, leaning on his elbows, "we should find out *why* Brad feels as he does. He's always seemed so open and outgoing."

"I know you like Brad. And you're right, he's normally not this way."

"Could he be jealous? He's probably made an effort to put what happened between you and your teenage boyfriend out of his mind, getting upset when reminded."

"I've wondered about that. I should have kept my feelings to myself. I shouldn't have insisted we talk about it."

"What's causing you anxiety now as your child's birthday approaches?"

"Remembering, I guess. Remembering the things that were going on in my life when I was her age. I was illegitimate, too, you know. I worry Abigail might follow in Mom's and my footsteps."

"You said the people who adopted her were Christians. Hopefully they raised Abigail with Christian values. Values you and your mother were deprived of."

He was watching Gail thoughtfully. "Are you wanting to find her? Wanting to establish a relationship with her?"

"No. When I gave her up I relinquished her completely to Kathy and Jim. I'd like to know how she is, though. You know, find out what's happening in her life."

"Do you think Brad might be worried you want her back?"

"I don't know. He won't let me talk to him long enough to find out what he thinks. I haven't been able to let him know that's the one thing I *don't* want."

She hesitated, then added, "I wasn't a Christian when I got pregnant. Or even when I gave my baby up. I came to the Lord afterward. But I still feel terrible about what I did."

"It's a good thing God finds it easier to forgive our sins than we do. You know, Gail, it comes down to unbelief. When we don't forgive ourselves after we've asked God's forgiveness, we're saying we don't believe in God's love and power." The man leaned forward again. "Do you recall the parable Jesus told about the prodigal son?"

"Yes. I know what you're getting at. The father forgave his son when he returned home. I believe God's forgiven me. Yet I still keep looking for a way to make up for what I did. That's one reason I want to work at the Crisis Pregnancy Center."

Tapping the Bible on his desk, Pastor Martin asked, "What did the prodigal son do to earn his father's favor when he returned home?"

"Well—nothing."

"That's right. God forgives without keeping score. As long as we're earnest when we ask forgiveness. Feeding on your guilt, looking for ways to make up for what you did, is like saying God can't or won't forgive you. You're sorrowing over something that's already been stamped 'Paid in full' in God's book."

She shook her head. "But that's not the only reason I want to work with the Center. When I took those baby clothes home I felt my energies being channeled away from me. I was doing something for the new mothers and their babies. It felt good. *I* felt good. Good about myself."

"You're positive you have no hidden reason for wanting to find out about your daughter?"

"I really don't. When I signed the adoption papers it was as though I was giving my child birth for the second time. The first was when she came into the world. The second was when she became a part of a complete family unit.

"That's another thing that bothers me. Shouldn't I be more troubled than I am over giving my child away? I mean, it doesn't seem natural. If I learned today where Abigail was, and had the opportunity to get her back, I wouldn't. Not unless she needed me."

Pastor Martin stared at her, an elbow braced on the arm of his chair, chin cradled between thumb and forefinger. "You honestly mean that, don't you?"

She scooted forward. "Yes. I do. Yet it makes me wonder about myself as a mother. As a woman. Shouldn't I want her? Is it normal to be willing to leave things as they are?"

"You're finding it hard to accept that you willingly let your daughter go?"

She looked at him, her dark eyes wide with realization. "Yes! That's it. I haven't been able to nail it down until now." She stared off at the corner of the room. "Maybe I lack normal mothering instincts."

"I'm sure you're a good mother, Gail. I'd imagine the Lord's the one shielding you from longing for your daughter. You should be grateful, not swamped by guilt. Be thankful for the peace God has granted."

He reached for his Bible, flipping it open to the first book of Samuel. Gail smiled when she saw the chapter. "The story of Hannah giving her son to Eli the priest. I've read it many times since becoming a Christian. It's helped me during these last fifteen years."

"But have you noticed the prayer Hannah offered before leaving the child with Eli? It's in the second chapter. She begins, 'My heart rejoices in the Lord; in the Lord my horn is lifted high.' "

He looked at Gail. "*Horn* here means strength. Hannah is saying that in the Lord she is strengthened. I believe this is what you've been experiencing. The Lord is holding you with his strength, sheltering you from the pain of having released your child."

"I've read that verse often," Gail admitted, "but I never saw it like that."

He ran a finger on down the page. "Here, in the last part of the third verse, Hannah says, 'The Lord is a God who knows, and by him deeds are weighed.' "

He looked at her again. "What does that say to you?"

Gail smiled, her face brightening. "That God knows the motives of my heart and actions. God knows I love my daughter and want what's best for her. Just as I do for Grant and Jimmy."

"I believe that's what our Lord is telling you, Gail. I believe God has shielded you from the intense pain of separating yourself from your daughter. God's led you to a husband who, despite his recent bad moods, loves you. And as with Hannah, God's given you other children. So you see, there's no need to feel guilty about being satisfied with things as they are."

The man leaned forward, pressing his fingertips together. "Now, about going against Brad by working at the Crisis Center."

She looked at him hopefully. "I'd really like to work with them."

"Maybe I should talk to Brad."

She shook her head. "I don't know—"

"Do you mind if I try?"

At last Gail agreed, wondering as she left how Brad would react knowing she had gone to their pastor. But before their minister could say a word to him, she found her husband had changed his mind again.

It happened that same evening. Brad came home saying that if Gail still wanted to volunteer at the Center, he wouldn't oppose her.

"I'm sorry I hurt you the other night," he added, shaking his head. "I'm sorry I left marks on your arm."

Gail called Pastor Martin the next morning asking

him not to say anything about their talk. She then called Mrs. Philips with the good news. It seemed things were finally smoothing out.

Thursday evening she announced she'd be starting evening classes the following week so she could answer the hot line from their home. "It won't take me out of the house, other than to counseling classes," she explained, hoping Brad was warming to the notion.

His face darkened. "What about the boys? In case I have to work late?"

"Mom keeps asking me to leave them with her. Besides, you've been coming home pretty regularly lately."

"You never know."

She wondered what he meant by that but wasn't about to ask. Hoping to appease him, she added, "I'm thinking of asking Mom and Tom over for dinner Saturday night. If that's okay."

"You know it is. But you're changing the subject."

Gail sighed. The air between them was icing again.

When she called her mother to invite them for dinner Saturday, she told Beverly of her plans to volunteer at the Center. Would Beverly mind watching the boys in case Brad had to work the nights she was in class?

"It would be fun! Tom enjoys the boys." Beverly added, "I've been thinking about the baby you gave away. Do you realize she's nearly the same age you were when she was born?"

So, her mother had been keeping track, too. "Yes. I know."

"There's a lot in my past I regret," Beverly admitted. "One is that I never got to see my granddaughter. We don't even have a picture of her. If I'd been a better mother and grandmother things might have turned out differently."

Gail couldn't argue with that.

Later she explained to Grant and Jimmy what she'd be doing. They listened quietly.

"How can girls have babies?" Jimmy asked.

"Yeah," Grant said, "I thought you had to get grown up first and be married before kids got born to you."

Gail nodded. "That's the way God meant it to be. But people don't always do things God's way. Like that time the two of you took off down the street when you were told not to leave the yard. Remember? You could have been hit by a car."

"I went cause Grant did," Jimmy alibied. "But we didn't have no babies 'cause we was bad."

Smiling, Gail pulled him onto her lap. "Not everyone has a baby when they do wrong. But for some girls that's what happens when they and their boyfriends do things meant only for married people. Can you understand that?"

Grant shook his head. "No. But that's okay. We're probably not old enough. That's what you tell us when we don't understand things."

She hugged her oldest, loving the old man in the little boy.

"What are you gonna do to help the girl mothers?" asked Jimmy, squirming around so he could look into her face.

She told them about the hot line and the classes she needed to take. "If I have to go to class when Dad's not home, I'll take you over to Grandma's to stay with her and Tom."

"Goody! Goody!" Jimmy enthused.

"Mom?" Grant was watching her. "How come you call Grandma, Grandma? But you call Grandpa Tom?"

"Because Tom's not my real father. He and Grandma just got married awhile back. Remember when we went to their wedding?"

"Yeah. So who *is* your father—our *real* grandpa?"

Closing her eyes briefly, Gail silently prayed for help.

"Mom?" Grant prodded.

"Honey, I don't know *where* my real father is. He didn't stay around long enough for me to get to know him."

"There's kids at school who live with just their moms or just their dads. Is that the way it was when you were little?"

She nodded, thanking the Lord the boy hadn't pressed the subject of *who* her father was. "Yes, that's the way it was."

"Are you and Dad gonna get a divorce?"

"Of course not! We love each other."

"No you don't!" countered Jimmy. "You been fightin'. Grant told me. He said—"

Gail stopped him. "Grant's not always right, even if he thinks he is. You and Grant don't always get along, but you still love each other. Right?"

Jimmy nodded, twisting around to look at his bother. "We do, don't we Grant?"

"I guess," his brother grudgingly agreed.

"That's the way it is with your dad and me. We don't always agree, but we still love each other."

But when Brad didn't come home for dinner the next night, not even calling to say he'd be late, Grant eyed her as though catching her in a lie. She ignored him, frightened something had happened to Brad, yet fearful Grant might be more right than she was willing to admit.

She was in the boys' room listening to their prayers

when they heard the car pull into the driveway. Grant smiled. "It's okay now, Mom. Dad's home."

But it wasn't okay. Brad was in the kitchen warming the plate of food in the microwave she had left in the refrigerator for him. He wouldn't look at her when she walked into the room.

"The boys were asking questions tonight, Brad. They're wondering if we're going to divorce."

He turned. "What do you expect *me* to do about it?"

Before she could think, she blurted out, "Go see Pastor Martin. Like I did."

"You told Pastor Martin about us?"

"Yes. I think we should both go to him."

"I'm not going for counseling with you, Gail."

"I told you awhile back I'd give up working at the Center if you'd tell me why you feel so strongly about it. But you said it was all right. Then after I get into it, you draw back again."

"It's just that you have enough to do, what with the boys, the house, your job—"

She went to him, encircling him with her arms, pressing her face against his chest. "I love you, Brad. Nothing's as important as that. Nothing. If you want me to give this up, I will."

He bent to kiss her before putting his hands on her shoulders to push her slightly away so he could look into her face. "I'll make a deal with you. If we don't have to talk about Abigail, I won't stand in your way. Go ahead and volunteer at the Center. As long as it doesn't hurt our family."

Gail stared at him. "Are you *sure* this time?"

His old teasing smile came back. "I think so."

So she began to attend evening classes, with Brad making a point of being home nights she was away. While he seemed to listen when she told him what she was learning, he seldom asked questions, appearing preoccupied.

The first evening Gail took a turn on the hot line Brad abruptly left the house. He returned a few hours later without explanation. Gail had received no calls. But it left her wondering. How would Brad have reacted if a call had come while he was home? The cycle was beginning again.

Gail was on the verge of throwing in the towel when he came home late one evening a week and a half before Christmas, gleefully declaring, "Grab your hat tight, Gail! Have I got news!"

"What is it? Good news, I hope."

He nodded. "I'd say so. I've found Abigail!"

# 5

## Good News?

Gail was staring at her husband. "You did what?"

"I've located Abigail. She's living in Eaton. Just fifty miles from here!"

Brad's joy was beyond Gail's understanding. She turned to make sure the boys hadn't heard, only to find them standing behind her in the doorway.

"Who's Abigail?" Grant asked, coming to stand beside his mother.

Brad glanced from son to wife. He crouched in front of Grant as Jimmy came closer. The younger boy went to him, hanging an arm around his father's neck. "Abigail's a girl your mother used to know. Mom hasn't seen her since the girl was a baby." He glanced at Gail and smiled. "I've found her and set up a time when she and your mother can meet again."

Gail couldn't believe—didn't *want* to believe— what she was hearing. "How *could* you?" she demanded, her throat tightening around her words.

He stood, his hand on Jimmy's head. "It was easy. I called Sue Grant to see if she recalled hearing what the girl's father did for a living. Sue said the attorney who handled—" he glanced at the boys, "—the matter mentioned Jim was planning to attend a Bible College somewhere in the state to study for the ministry.

"You had said their first names were Jim and Kathy, so I gave the editor of our religious page my phone credit card and asked him to contact the Bible colleges around the state. I told him to check on an older student who might have attended fifteen years ago by the first name of Jim or James. Someone who had a wife named either Kathy or Katherine."

"And he found them? With no more information than that?"

"He did. The registrar of the third college he called had attended classes with Jim. They got to know each other well. I called the registrar and asked if Jim had a daughter. The man told me Jim and Kathy adopted a baby girl just before Jim entered college."

"Did you tell him why you wanted to know?"

Brad shook his head. "No, I told him I was with *The Linden Globe* and needed to get in touch with Jim but didn't know his last name. He not only gave me Jim's name but the church he's pastoring near here. I called then and talked to him. He—"

Gail put up a hand. "Wait. I can't take this in so fast. Besides," she glanced at the boys, "I think we'd better wait until after dinner."

"Yeah," agreed Jimmy, "I'm hungry."

"Come on, boys. Let's wash our hands," Brad said, striding from the room as though walking on air.

As Gail turned back to the stove her hands were trembling.

Grant had hung back. He stood silently watching,

then asked, "Did Dad know this girl, too?"

"No." Gail shook her head. "I didn't meet your father until after her parents took her away."

"Is she somebody special?"

"Yes."

"Are me and Jimmy special, too?"

Was her son catching on? Fear seemed to shade his eyes. Would she have to tell them? She tried to smile. "You and Jimmy are very special to me and your dad. You always will be. But there are other people who also have special places in our lives. Everyone's special in their own way."

"I just called your mom," Brad announced as he and Jimmy came back to the kitchen. "I asked if we could bring the boys by tonight so we could go Christmas shopping. I figured that would be all right with you." Heading Grant toward the bathroom to wash, Brad lowered his voice. "It'll give us a chance to talk."

"Has Grandma bought some more new toys?" Jimmy asked.

His father sighed. "I wish your grandmother would stop buying you things all the time."

"But that's what grandmas do!" protested Jimmy.

Gail found it almost impossible to eat. She noticed Grant having trouble, too, shifting his food from one side of the plate to the other. Finally she asked, "Aren't you anxious to go to Grandma and Grandpa's tonight?"

He shrugged listlessly. "I s'ppose."

She was moving, saying, doing things mechanically. She must not, she told herself, allow her feelings to surface until the boys were safely at her mother's. Raw hope at the prospect of seeing her daughter mixed with fear of seeing her.

Outwardly Gail appeared in control. She had to, for Grant's sake. He was growing far too wise for his age. But all the while a quiet rage was building toward Brad for not consulting her. How dare he interfere in Abigail's life! All her good intentions were being wrenched from her.

As they walked back to the car after leaving the boys with her mother and Tom, Brad asked, "Where do you want to go?"

"Home! I want to go home."

She said nothing all the drive back. Once inside she walked quietly to the living room. "Start from the beginning, Brad. Tell me again what you've done."

He did, adding, "Their last name is Marshal. Reverend and Mrs. James Marshal. They came to Eaton several months ago after pastoring a church in the south."

"Was Jim surprised to hear from you? Did he sound angry? Happy? What?"

"Well, happy's not the word. Fearful, maybe."

"Did you tell him I had nothing to do with locating them?"

Brad nodded.

"And you set a time we're to meet with them? Including Abigail?"

"Yes. We'll be seeing her and her parents together."

Gail got to her feet. "I'm going to fix myself a cup of tea. Do you want some?"

"Sounds good. But I'll get it."

"No! I'd like to be alone for a few minutes."

She stood staring out the kitchen window while the water heated. Forgotten toy trucks awaited their absentee owners in the back as darkness staked its claim to the yard. What sort of toys had her little girl played with when she was younger? What was she like now? How would she react to seeing her real mother?

Gail brought herself up short. She wasn't the girl's *real* mother. She was her natural mother. Her birth mother. Kathy, the slim, blond, Swedish-looking woman she'd met at the hospital after Abigail was born, was the girl's *real* mother. *And don't you forget it, Gail Lorring! Not ever!*

Carrying the hot mugs of tea back to the living room, Gail placed Brad's on the coffee table in front of him. Purposely she moved to the other side across from her husband. She cupped her hands around her mug and took a sip, watching him over the rim.

"Brad. I don't know what to say other than I'm far from happy. I never meant to try to find my daughter. If she had looked for me it would be different. But to interfere in her life, all of their lives, as you've done—"

"I don't understand you, Gail. You've been moaning around, groaning on and on about your long lost daughter, pinning my ears to the wall for not being concerned about your feelings. Then when I do something to help, you accuse me of interfering. What's with you, anyway?"

"I could ask you the same. You refuse to discuss the baby I gave up. Then you flip-flop. Why?"

He merely shrugged. "I'd hoped to bring peace to our lives by doing something for you. I thought you'd be happy. I had no idea you didn't want to get in touch with Abigail. You never gave me a clue."

"Because," she leaned forward pointing a finger, "you never let me talk about it."

Gail slumped against the high backed upholstered chair. "I've been thinking about what you said when we met—when I first told you I'd had a baby when I was a teenager. Do you remember that night beside the camp fire?"

He nodded. "I remember we talked long into the night. I listened to all you had to say."

"You did. And you've never been judgmental. You told me I should be proud of carrying my baby to term. Then you said we'd never talk about it again."

"So?" he questioned. "I didn't think there was anything more to be said."

Brad rose, walking toward their bedroom. His face was livid. Turning on his heel he came back to stand in front of her. "So what do we do now? We're suppose to meet the Marshals two weeks from Saturday. Between Christmas and New Years. Jim asked for time to get through Christmas before telling Abigail. What do we do now?"

"I really don't know, Brad. I'll have to think about it. Pray about it."

She was thoughtful for a time, then looked up. "Maybe I should call Kathy. See what she has to say."

There was a brooding lull between them as they drove back to pick the boys up. Gail wondered aloud if she should tell them about Abigail before Grant and Jimmy caught on to what was happening.

Brad offered no opinion other than, "That's for you to decide since I've already committed the unforgivable sin."

Gail moved through the next two days as though veiled from reality. Her mind and body functioned on automatic, while her imagination ran ahead searching for answers. The problem was she didn't know the proper questions. Part of her wanted to see Abigail. Part of her wanted to hide. Could she meet her daughter, then walk away from her again? She wasn't sure. And what of Jim and Kathy?

At last the weekend arrived. Early Saturday Beverly called. "What time are you picking me up?"

Not wanting to admit she'd forgotten her agreement to take her mother Christmas shopping, Gail started to beg off, then decided not to. Brad had planned to spend the day with Grant and Jimmy—men's day out—while Gail took Beverly shopping.

On the drive to the mall Beverly chattered like a little girl. Gail was used to nodding and uh-huhing in all the right places as the boys rambled on while her mind wandered. Now she did the same with her mother.

A bell ringer opened the door when they reached the mall entrance. Gail started inside then glanced back as her mother dropped coins in the metal pot before hurrying to catch up. Brightly decorated Christmas trees were displayed in the common. Shoppers pushed past as Gail and Beverly headed toward one of the larger department stores.

But as Gail reached the store she realized her mother was lagging again. Turning, she saw Beverly talking to a woman with a child in a stroller. The youngster was dressed all in pink. Ooze from a sticky candy cane dripped from the youngster's chin.

Gail waited and watched. In the old days her mother would have walked by the child without noticing. Gratitude for the change struck Gail. She had been witnessing it all along, but until that moment hadn't acknowledged the transformation that had taken place since her mother stopped drinking.

Beverly picked out a jacket for Tom as Gail tried unsuccessfully to push away memories of Christmases past. Like when she was ten. Her mother had been drinking and couldn't remember where she had put the gifts she said she had bought. Sodden with liquor, Beverly had begged Gail to forgive her.

And then there had been the Christmas Gail spent

at the Salvation Army home, baby-bloated and miserable, trying to decide what to do when her child was born. Her mother hadn't remembered her that year, either.

Gail tried to shut the door on those old raw hurts as she trailed her mother from store to store. Beverly picked out some toys, then asked Gail's advice on clothes for the boys.

Finally Beverly asked, "Aren't you doing any shopping?"

"Guess I'm just not in the mood."

"Christmas is less than a week and a half away."

"I know. Let's stop and eat lunch. Maybe I'll be able to shove my mind into gear afterward."

Gail deliberately chose a quiet corner of a less frequented restaurant. She dug her gift list from her purse, glanced at it, then looked up at her mother. "I've had a lot on my mind lately. Sorry to be such a rotten shopping companion."

"Want to talk about it?"

"Yes. If you don't mind. It's about your granddaughter—" Gail told her all that had been happening.

Throughout the telling Beverly's eyes grew large. Absentmindedly she pushed her hair back from her face as she listened. Gail noted the pain in her mother's eyes. She was no doubt recalling her own part in the story. Finally Beverly took a tissue from her purse and dabbed at her eyes.

Gail finished and sat back exhausted, staring across the narrow table at her mother.

"Could I go with you to see her?" Beverly asked, reaching for Gail's hand.

Gail hadn't considered that her mother might want to go along. She shook her head. "I don't think that would be a good idea. I'm not even sure *I* should see her. I gave her up, Mom. She has a mother and father now. They're the only parents Abigail's ever known."

"Of course you should see her! She's *your* daughter, after all!" Then glancing away, her voice barely audible, Beverly added, "But then I have no right telling you what a mother should or shouldn't do."

"Mom, it's okay. I've forgiven you. You weren't yourself while you were drinking."

"It still hurts, Gail. Just like having to give your baby up hurts you."

"It doesn't hurt like it did," Gail admitted.

Beverly dabbed at her eyes again. "I wish you'd been able to keep her. I wish I'd been able to help the two of you."

Gail reached over to push a strand of hair back from her mother's face, noticing how pretty she was without the thick makeup she used to wear. The hard brittle lines had softened.

When they left the restaurant they found neither had a heart for shopping. Gail dropped Beverly off then drove on home to find Brad and the boys still gone. She took the opportunity to call Jenny.

"I knew something was bothering you the last few days when you picked the boys up," Jenny acknowledged when Gail told her about Brad locating Abigail. "You don't feel you should see the girl, do you?"

"No. I don't. She's not mine, Jen. She's not a something you own. That's what I told Jim and Kathy before they look her."

"Do you have any idea how Abigail feels about all this?"

"Not a clue. We haven't heard from the Marshals since Brad talked to Jim on the phone."

As soon as she hung up Gail dialed Sue Grant's number. Sue wasn't at home, but Mack was. Gail told him what had happened and asked him to have Sue call.

"We'll be praying for you, Gail," Mack offered. "You just hang in. Don't let it get to you. You hear?"

Gail nodded, forgetting he couldn't see her. "Thanks."

She was thinking about calling Pastor Martin for an appointment. But Brad returned just then with the boys. They too had been shopping.

"We got you a present!" Jimmy shouted, throwing himself against her. "But I can't tell you it's a robe."

"Shut up," Grant warned. "You just told her!"

Jimmy pulled back looking puzzled. "No I didn't. I said I couldn't tell."

Gail smoothed her younger son's hair. "I really wasn't listening. Besides, if I had heard, I still wouldn't know what color it was."

"It's—"

Grant put a quick hand over his brother's mouth while commenting. "You been forgetting to listen to a lot of things lately, Mom."

Glancing at Brad over their sons' heads, she responded, "I guess I have. I'm sorry."

"Dad says you been thinking about seeing that girl Abigail you used to know." He rattled around in the packages he was carrying, pulling out a bright red and brown patterned scarf. "We bought this for her our own selves. For Christmas."

Gail didn't know what to say. Brad finally came to her rescue. "Take the packages to your room. I'll come later to help you wrap them."

The two trudged off as Gail turned to Brad. "What was all that about?"

"Grant's worried about Abigail. He asked if we ever wished he or Jimmy had been girls. He said, 'Like Abigail and Jenny who has a boy *and* a girl.'"

"What did you tell him?"

"Just that we were happy with our family the way it was. Then Jimmy asked if they could buy Abigail a present. I thought it might make them feel more a part of what was going on."

"They may never get to see her. I don't want them with us when we meet her. *If* we meet her."

"I told them we'd give Abigail their gift. And that Grandma probably had something special planned for them that day."

"Good. I've let Mom in on what's happening. She asked if she could go along, but I told her no. Maybe it will satisfy her knowing we need her help with the boys while we're gone that day."

"I'm hungry," Jimmy announced, bounding back into the room.

While Brad herded the boys off to the parking lot, Gail waited after church the next day to speak to Pastor Martin. "I need to talk to you. Soon."

Pastor Martin pulled a small notebook from an inside pocket. "How about Tuesday morning at nine? You aren't working that day, are you?"

She shook her head. "Tuesday is fine. I have to drive down to the Crisis Pregnancy Center that morning anyway. I'll stop on my way."

# 6

## A Sister Discovered

Brad suggested they stop for hamburgers on the way home from church. The boys cast their votes for the Burger Palace. More for the inside play area than for the quality of food, Gail knew. Grant and Jimmy headed for the tall, twisting tube slide after eating most of their hamburgers.

"I think," Brad said, turning to Gail, "we'd better spend as much time with them as we can. Especially now. I don't know what's going on in our oldest son's head, but something has him up a tree."

"It's hard to tell how much he understands. Or guesses."

"Should we tell him? Tell them both they have a half sister?"

Gail was shaking her head. "No. Not yet. I'm still not sure I should see her."

Brad stared at his wife but said nothing.

As soon as they arrived home Brad sent the boys to

their room to change clothes. He then pulled a box containing a model airplane from a bag of Christmas gifts hidden in the hall closet.

"What on earth are you doing?" Gail whispered, glancing at the boy's room. "They'll be out any minute."

"I'm going to give this to them now. They don't need to know it was for Christmas. It will give us something to do as a family this afternoon."

Gail smiled. "Sure, Brad! You've been wanting to get your hands on that model since we bought it."

Brad had the coffee table cleared and the box sitting on it by the time the boys came back.

"Wow!" Jimmy breathed.

"That's pretty neat, Dad. Is it for us?" Grant asked.

Gail watched from the couch as the three sat on the floor around the low coffee table, dissecting tiny pieces from long plastic stems.

"Want to help?" Brad invited.

"No thanks. I'll watch." She was sure they wouldn't miss her.

After awhile she wandered to the kitchen and looked out the window. It was starting to rain. Having her family together in the dry warmth of the house would normally have warmed Gail. Not today. Not while agonizing over Abigail. Not while wondering what she should do about meeting with the Marshals.

Vividly she recalled the tiny newborn she had seen only once through the hospital's nursery room window before they took her away. What would she look like now?

The phone rang. Gail picked up the receiver to find it was Sue Grant. Keeping her voice low, Gail told Sue about Brad's search for Abigail and the meeting he had set up.

"Please pray for us, Sue," Gail whispered.

After hanging up she went back to the living room, stopping to watch the progress on the model.

"Who was that?" Brad asked without looking up.

"Here," Grant said to his father. "I found the red piece that goes on the one you just picked up."

"Sue Grant, returning a call I made to her yesterday while she was out."

Brad pushed another part toward Jimmy. "See if you can fit this onto the one you have."

At last Gail went to her bedroom, softly closing the door. She sat on the edge of the bed and picked up her Bible. It seemed to open by itself to the familiar passage in Samuel. As she reread the story of Hannah, Gail especially noted woman's return home with her husband and younger children after her yearly visit with Samuel.

Gail closed her eyes. Could she be that brave? Could she see her daughter, then return home content to leave things as they were? What had Samuel thought of the woman who had given him away? Especially after leaving him each year to return home with his younger brothers and sisters. Had he understood why Hannah didn't take him with her?

What about Abigail? How would the girl react to seeing her birth mother for the first time, this woman who also now had other children?

Slipping to her knees, Gail buried her face in the thick quilting of the bedspread. "God in heaven, guide me. I don't know what I should do. I'm not nearly as courageous as Hannah. I don't want to hurt anyone. Not Abigail, Jim, Kathy, my husband, or our boys. And what about my mother?"

Gail's mind drifted back over the years as she poured her frustrations and pain out to her Lord and

Savior. She lost track of time as she remained on her knees, not even hearing the bedroom door open and close as Brad entered. He placed a gentle hand on her shoulder. Gail looked up as Brad knelt beside her.

"Lord," he began, "we need your guidance as we prepare to meet this girl and her family." He prayed on, seeking help for them all. When finished he helped Gail to her feet.

She stood staring into the blue-green of his eyes for a moment before speaking. "Honey, I don't want to keep that appointment."

Brad stepped back, scowling. "Don't you realize how fortunate you are this child is alive so you *can* see her? Think of the women who have aborted their babies. Many still agonizing."

"What has that got to do with my seeing Abigail?"

"You ought to be grateful the girl lives."

"Honey, I am."

"I think you'd better know what happened out there in the living room before I came to find you."

Wary, Gail sank down on the edge of the bed.

Brad stood there, an arm braced on the dresser top. "I told Grant and Jimmy about Abigail."

"That's what I was afraid you were going to say."

"I had to. Grant was asking questions. It seems he was awake the other morning and overheard us. He asked why—if he has a sister—we've hidden her."

"Oh, no!" Gail breathed.

"It gets worse. He's wondering if we're going to give him and Jimmy away, too."

Gail buried her face in her hands and wept. "The poor little guy. I knew something was wrong, something was bothering him. But I didn't realize—"

"I had to tell him. Both of them," Brad emphasized.

She nodded.

"As far as I can see, you have no choice about seeing Abigail." He sat beside her and reached for her hand. "If we ignore Abigail's existence now, the boys will think we might someday turn from them."

"You didn't manipulate the conversation just so you could tell them, did you? And by telling them, force me to see her?"

"Are you accusing me of lying?" he demanded, suddenly on his feet again. He stood there as though about to say something, then changed his mind. He walked to the door. "You'd better come talk to them."

Gail wiped her eyes before following him to the living room.

Jimmy was still poking around at the model parts. Grant sat slouched on the couch, kicking the front with the heel of a shoe. Gail took a deep breath as she sat beside her eldest son. His body stiffened as she pulled him against her. At last he looked up, tears rimming his eyes.

"I understand Dad told you about Abigail."

Grant nodded. "I already knew. She's our sister isn't she? Jimmy's and mine."

"She's your half sister. That means she has a different father than you and Jimmy."

The younger boy scooted across the floor to rest his cheek on his mother's knee. "Dad told us you had Abigail before you had us."

"That's right. I was a very young girl when Abigail was born. Too young to know much about babies." She glanced at Brad. "I was wrong in not waiting to have a baby until after I met and married your father. I had a boy friend then. And—well, we did things meant only for married people to do. I got pregnant. Abigail was born when I was only fifteen."

"That's really pretty old, though," Jimmy noted, his eyes wide and knowing.

Gail shook her head. "Not old enough to take good care of a tiny, helpless, little baby. Remember, I wasn't living with my mother—your grandmother—then. Some parents are able to help their teenage girls keep their babies. But Grandma couldn't do that for me since she was sick much of the time."

Leaning toward his brother, Grant told him, "Grandma used to get drunk a lot."

Gail glanced at Grant and nodded. "So I turned my baby over to a nice couple who had no children. They had been praying for a baby. I could tell they loved Abigail from the moment they saw her."

"Did you cry when they took her away?" Grant asked, somewhat hopefully.

"Yes." She squeezed him closer. "And many many times since. But I knew the people would take good care of her."

"Do you love me and Grant as much as you loved her?" Jimmy inquired.

She smiled. "You know I love you. So very very much." She looked down into Grant's upturned face.

"I'll never forget the first time I saw each of you after you were born. I'd hold you and hold you, not wanting the nurse to take you back to the nursery. You two were mine to raise. You're so special to me."

Slowly a smile relaxed Grant's face. "I'm glad!"

"Me too," Gail said, hugging him tight as she pulled Jimmy onto her lap. "The Lord gave me two wonderful little boys to love. For that I thank him everyday." She looked at one and then the other. "Do you remember the Bible story about Samuel? How Samuel's mother, Hannah, took him to God's house to live while he was still a little boy?"

They shook their heads.

"Well then, I think we'd better get your Bible storybook right now so we can read it together."

Grant asked later, as Brad and Gail heard their bedtime prayers, "Can we go with you to see our sister?"

"I'm afraid not. Not this time." But would there ever be a second time? Gail wondered.

"She'd probably boss us around," Jimmy noted. "Like Kim does sometimes when we play at her house after school?"

"I hardly think so," Gail told him. "Abigail won't be living with us like a real sister. She has her own adoptive parents now."

But as Gail and Brad were leaving the boys' room, Brad remarked, "You never know, honey. Someday Abigail might become part of our family. It would be kind of nice, wouldn't it?"

Gail motioned Brad toward the kitchen. Once there she turned to face him. "I don't understand the change in you. You wouldn't talk to me about Abigail a few days ago. Now that's all you want to talk about. I used to wonder if you were jealous I was intimate with someone else before we met."

Brad drew in a deep breath, slowly shaking his head. "I won't pretend it's never bothered me. It's just that I felt it was better to try to forget. But when I saw what it was doing to you—to us—I decided I'd better try to locate the girl."

Gail felt there was still something he wasn't telling. Pressing him, however, seemed to do no good. "You're not thinking we should try to take her away from Jim and Kathy, are you?"

"You never know what may come of this. She may want to spend some time with us."

Linking her arm through his, Gail pressed her face against Brad's shoulder. "It would be nice. But she's not mine, you know. She's not someone you own."

Tuesday morning Gail kept her appointment with Pastor Martin. She told him about Brad finding the girl, scheduling the meeting with the Marshals, then telling the boys about their half sister.

"What do you suppose caused Brad's change?"

Gail offered a tired shrug. "I have no idea."

"Has he explained his reluctance to your working at the Crisis Pregnancy Center?"

"No. The last time we argued about it was just before he found Abigail. Maybe he regretted his attitude. Maybe he found her to try to make it up to me."

"Possibly. It sounds as though you've handled the situation with the boys pretty well. How have they been since learning about their sister?"

"Good. They're still curious. But Grant doesn't seem as troubled as he was."

Pastor Martin nodded. "Children in the home have a way of sensing when things aren't right." He rubbed his chin. "You're still having misgivings about seeing the girl?"

"Yes. I suppose we have to go through with it, but I'm not at all sure it's right. All I ever wanted was to make sure she was happy and not making the same mistakes I made. I'm praying for guidance, but so far I see no clear direction."

"Are you reading your Bible, Gail?"

She nodded. "And reading again about Hannah."

"Did you know there's another person in the Bible who willingly gave up a child?"

"You mean God? When he gave his Son Jesus to reclaim us?"

"Actually, I was thinking of someone else. Abraham."

"Oh. The time God told him to sacrifice his son Isaac."

The man nodded.

"But the Lord was only testing Abraham. God never intended to let him go through with it."

"No. But Abraham didn't know that. Yet he was willing to do what God asked."

"I wasn't a Christian when I released Abigail for adoption. So I can't pretend I was trying to do God's will."

"Maybe not. But your Christian foster mother had a lot to do with your decision, according to what you told me last time."

Gail agreed. "Are you suggesting God may be about to give my daughter back to me? Like God returned Isaac?"

"I'm not suggesting anything. Other than God gives us courage and strength to carry out his plans for us." The man leaned comfortably in his chair. "How are you feeling about your mother now?"

"That's the one area that's working out. I realize she loved me all along. It was her drinking that short-circuited everything."

Gail started to rise, then stopped. "You seem to feel I should see Abigail."

"You've got to do what you think is best. What's right for all in God's sight. Although I agree with Brad about the boys. They might be hurt if you turned your back on the girl now. All kinds of questions could come to their minds."

He prayed with her, then she left. On the drive home Gail realized she was feeling better about things. Circumstances, God—she wasn't sure which—seemed to be pushing her toward meeting the Marshals in just a week and a half.

Having decided to keep the appointment, Gail threw herself into Christmas preparations. There was the tree to buy and put up. Cookies to bake. Gifts to finish buying and wrapping. She invited her mother and Tom over for Christmas Eve. Beverly asked them for Christmas dinner.

She had put off doing any more for the Crisis Pregnancy Center until after New Year's. By then she hoped she'd have Brad's blessing.

They squeezed the church Christmas program into their busy schedules the Sunday evening before Christmas. As promised, Beverly and Tom went with them. Gail kept stealing glances at her mother, who was sitting with Tom in the pew beside them.

Brad jabbed her in the ribs. "What are you doing?" he whispered. "The program is up on the platform."

Gail smiled sheepishly. "I was watching Mom. I've never seen her like this. Did you notice her pointing Grant and Jimmy out to the people on the other side of them?"

Brad whispered, "She's just being a grandma."

Gail kept busy the day after Christmas while at home with Grant and Jimmy. The boys occupied themselves with their new toys in the morning while she caught up on her household tasks. She then read to them after lunch.

Beverly continued to be disappointed she couldn't go with Gail to meet the granddaughter she had never seen. Yet she remained a good sport, assuring her daughter she'd do all she could to keep the boys busy while Gail and Brad were at Eaton.

# 7

## *Face-to-Face*

As their appointment with the Marshals edged closer, Gail's anxiety deepened. Brad, on the other hand, became more like the man she had married. It was the closest they had been in weeks. She sensed his excitement at seeing the girl. He asked what Gail's baby had looked like when she was born, what Gail had said to the Marshals before they took the baby away, how much they had revealed about themselves.

Grant and Jimmy asked some questions after being told they had a half sister, then accepted it as normal since it was no longer a mystery.

"Lots of kids have sisters and brothers they don't live with," Jimmy pointed out one morning.

"Yeah," Grant agreed, "it's no big deal."

Gail dressed carefully that Saturday morning. Thoughts and memories chased through her mind as she took off the black suit and pink blouse she had first chosen. She looked through her closet, finally deciding on a simple, rust-colored knit dress with a wide black belt, draping a black and rust scarf over one shoulder.

She hesitated in front of the floor-length mirror. She was still slim, even though she had given birth to three children. Her appearance was much as it had been fifteen years before, when she first met Jim and Kathy. Gail realized with relief she was more self-assured than that depressed, mixed-up teenager who had released her baby for adoption.

"Accept—" she breathed aloud. "Accept for today."

The Lord had been with her every step of the way and would be with her today, she was sure. She would continue to trust him even though the day promised to be the most difficult since she said good-bye to her infant daughter so many years ago.

After one last look in the mirror, Gail picked up her purse. She took a deep breath, then stepped out to face a day chilled by wind blowing briskly under heavy gray clouds.

They dropped the boys off at Beverly and Tom's apartment. Then Brad turned the car onto the wet freeway toward Eaton. Jim had called Brad at work two days before, informing him they had chosen a friend's house for their meeting.

The fifty miles passed quickly. Too quickly for Gail. As they entered the small town Brad glanced at his watch. "We're half an hour early. Want to stop for coffee?"

She shook her head.

He reached over to hold her hand as he turned the car into a grocery store parking lot and turned the motor off. "Are you okay?

"I think so." She sighed, her pale face making her dark eyes look larger than usual. "Are you sure we're not doing wrong?"

"We have every right to see our child."

"*Our* child? It's nice you're able to think of her that way. But you're not the one responsible for her birth."

Laughing, Brad slipped an arm around Gail. "Community property, you know, honey. What's mine is yours and vice-versa."

Twenty minutes dragged by before he started the motor. He drove to the end of Main and turned left, stopping before a green, ranch-style house with a wide front lawn. As Gail looked toward the house she noticed someone near the window move out of sight.

Her mouth went dry. Her hands turned clammy as she reached for the door handle. "I guess this is it."

Brad opened his own door with an eagerness belying his earlier quiet reflections. Gail's legs felt wooden as they walked through the chilled damp wind to the front door. Brad pressed the bell button. A full minute passed before the door opened and a man stood before them.

Could this be Jim? Gail wondered. He seemed so much older. His hair was steel gray now. Although his eyes were the intense blue she remembered. Behind him waited Kathy, still tall and willowy. Her hair was shorter now, the blond fading to white.

"Come in," Jim invited, standing out of the way. "Our friends left the house to us for the morning."

Gail managed to smile at Kathy, who also appeared tense. Brad followed his wife into the house as Jim closed the door. Gail was turning back toward Brad when her eyes caught sight of a girl. *The* girl.

"You've hardly changed, Gail," Kathy was saying.

But Gail scarcely heard. Slumped in a large overstuffed chair was her daughter. She had on jeans, a pink sweatshirt, and scuffed white tennis shoes.

Her daughter! Steve's and her daughter. There was

no mistaking the resemblance. It was as though Gail still stood in front of her bedroom mirror. There were the same dark eyes in the oval face framed by an equally dark mane of thick chestnut hair.

"This is Abby," Jim said. "*Our* daughter."

Gail recognized the emphasis on *our*. She remembered Brad's own *our* just minutes before.

"I could have guessed this was Abigail," Brad said. To the girl he added, "You look so much like our oldest son!"

"My name's Abby. It has *never* been Abigail," she admonished, pouting.

Kathy moved to sit on the arm of the girl's chair. She placed a motherly hand on her adopted daughter's shoulder. "We named her Abby Marie. It seemed to fit better than Abigail."

*And eliminated my name from hers,* Gail thought. She turned toward Jim, making a feeble attempt at conversation. "I understand you're a minister now."

He nodded stiffly.

"I didn't know Brad had begun a search for Abigail—I mean, for Abby."

"It surprised us, too," Jim admitted.

"Won't you both sit down?" Kathy motioned to a couch.

"Thank you." Gail sat with Brad beside her. He reached for her hand. She wasn't sure why, but she pulled it from his. She turned slightly toward Abby, in time to catch the girl staring at her. Their eyes met before Abby looked away.

Brad cleared his throat. "Gail has worried our visit would disrupt your lives."

"Then why are you here?" Abby demanded, her tone raw. "I knew I was adopted. Mom and Dad told me when I was little. I sure don't need any more parents than I already have."

Gail's breath caught as she searched Kathy's eyes for a hint of understanding. She turned to the girl again. "Abby, I'm not here to hurt you. But after Brad found you, and we learned you lived so close—"

"Dad says you've got other kids now. You don't need me!"

Gail wanted to say, *Oh, but I do need you. At least your understanding.* But she didn't.

"What do you hope to gain by seeing Abby?" Jim asked.

Gail closed her eyes, trying to think how to respond.

"Peace of mind," Brad replied for her. "That's what I'd like for Gail. During the last few months she's been consumed wondering about her daughter."

"*Our* daughter!" Jim corrected. "Abby has been our daughter from the minute we carried her out of the hospital. We're the ones who comforted her when she was teething, saw her through her childhood illnesses, went with her to her first day of school."

Abby rose to face Gail. "What have *you* done for me, besides give me away to be rid of me?"

Brad again rose to Gail's defense. "I'll tell you what Gail *didn't* do, Abby. She didn't abort you. She safeguarded you through pregnancy, disrupted her own life, risked her reputation."

The girl's eyes flashed as she turned on him. "Lots of girls keep their babies. They don't all have abortions. But your wife didn't even try." She looked again at Gail. "Don't get me wrong. I'm thankful for the parents I have. What it really comes down to is—you didn't want me."

Jim moved to Abby's side as though to quiet her. But the girl pulled away, continuing her tongue-lashing. "Now you show up and I'm supposed to feel something for you?"

"No. Of course not." Gail shook her head, her voice choked. "I just wanted to be sure you were all right."

Kathy moved to the couch beside Gail. "Abby has been a good child. A contented baby. She's just upset at the moment. Although her teen years *are* proving a bit rough." Kathy glanced at Jim and Abby. "But together we'll pull through."

The next thing Gail knew Brad was on his feet, reaching into a back pocket. The old familiar grin spread across his face. "How would you like to see pictures of your half brothers? You'll be amazed how much you look like our oldest son."

The girl didn't reply at once, glancing first at Jim. "I—I guess it wouldn't hurt," she finally conceded.

Jim nodded. "I'd like to see them."

Brad pulled snapshots from his billfold. Love for him washed over Gail as the tension in the room eased.

Soon all but Gail stood with Brad looking at the photos. Gail was as miserable as she had ever been. Those old sensations of rejection were back, wrapping her in a cocoon of hurt.

Spontaneous laughter startled Gail from her remorse. Abby was holding a picture out to her. "This one is great!"

Brad turned to Gail. "It's the one of Jimmy dressed like a cowboy, sneaking up on the neighbor's cat with a rope."

"I didn't know you had those with you." She stood to look at the picture the girl held out to her as Kathy drew Gail into their circle.

"By the way. Where's that Christmas gift the boys bought for Abby?" Brad inquired.

"It's here." Gail reached for her purse. She gave the small, gift-wrapped scarf to Abby, who opened it on the spot.

The girl looked at the scarf, then carefully folded the wrapping paper back around it. "Tell them I said thanks."

"We might as well sit down," Jim said. To Kathy he added, "Why don't you bring the coffee in?"

Kathy headed for the kitchen shadowed by Abby, leaving Jim alone with Gail and Brad. "I need to apologize," Jim said. "Abby and I have been a bit hard on you, I'm afraid. She's mixed up. She doesn't know how she should feel or behave around you. As a matter of fact, Kathy and I have been having the same difficulty. But I suppose you've noticed."

He leaned forward, his eyes holding Gail's. "You're a Christian, aren't you Gail?"

"Yes. Although I wasn't when Abby was born."

"You have two terrific looking boys. Are you happy?"

Gail nodded again, glancing at Brad.

"We've been nervous about this meeting," he continued. "I've prayed about it, but I'm only human. People seem to think ministers are above such feelings. We're not. At least *I'm* not."

"I've wanted to call the whole thing off," Gail told him. "But I was afraid Abby would wonder why I didn't want to see her."

"Then," Brad added, "our boys overheard us talking. We had to tell them about her. Grant got it into his head we might give *them* away too. We were really in a bind then. If we hadn't come, they might have felt a mother who didn't care about her first born would someday not care about them."

Jim was slowly nodding his head. "That could be a problem."

"It's my fault for stirring up the whole mess," Brad admitted. "I should have talked to Gail before trying to find you."

Jim reached into a pocket. "Would you like to see pictures of Abby when she was younger?"

"Oh, yes," Gail replied eagerly.

Kathy returned alone with a tray of cookies and a coffeepot. She set the tray on an end table, then poured them each coffee.

"Where's Abby?" Jim wondered.

"She'll be out in a minute." Turning to Brad and Gail, Kathy asked, "Please tell us what you expect from us and our daughter. She really is *our* daughter, you know."

"Yes," Gail responded, "She is. But lately I've been so concerned. Especially as her fifteenth birthday approached. I was fifteen, you know, when she was born. I've been praying she won't make the mistakes I made at her age."

"I had forgotten," Jim noted. "You *were* Abby's age when she was born, weren't you?"

"I was also illegitimate. I don't want my child following in my mother's and my footsteps. I needed to be certain things were better for her."

Jim and Kathy glanced at one another, then looked away.

"Is something wrong?" Gail asked.

Kathy was rubbing her palms together. "It's just that—well, she has a boyfriend. A boy we don't completely trust."

Jim sighed. "I'm afraid being a preacher's daughter hasn't been easy for her, what with moving from church to church and town to town, always having to make new friends. Abby's quite strong-willed."

Chuckling, Brad glanced at Gail. "I know what you mean! My wife and oldest son have the same tendency."

Abby returned at that moment. She picked up a

cookie and sat down, nibbling as she watched Gail through half closed eyes.

"Our church is sending us to a mission outpost in Mexico for three months," Jim was saying. "A couple of other families are going along. One of the women is a retired teacher, so Abby will be able to keep up with her schooling. We're leaving in two weeks."

"Yeah," Abby said. "They think I'll forget Cody."

"Who's Cody?" Gail asked, wondering if the Marshals had concocted the trip after Brad got in touch with them.

"A boy I know."

"Oh—is he nice?"

"He is to me."

Brad asked Jim, "When do you expect to be back?"

"About the middle of April. Just before Abby's birthday."

"I was hoping we could see you again before too long. I'd like Abby to meet our sons. Gail's mother would like to meet her, too. My mother-in-law stopped drinking and has turned out to be a neat lady. Maybe you could come to our house for dinner before you leave?"

Gail was shaking her head. "No, Brad. Not unless *they* want to."

"I don't think we should rush this," Kathy said. She turned to her daughter. "I believe Abby needs more time. I know I do."

"Tell you what," Brad said. "When you get back from Mexico, I'll give Abby a big family birthday party. We'll have it at The Towers, the best restaurant in Linden."

Seeming pleased with himself, Brad looked from one to the other. He received only cold stares until his eyes rested on Abby.

"For me?"

"For you!"

"Brad, I don't think—" Gail stopped, not knowing what to say. How could she protest in front of Abby?

Jim took up where Gail left off. "I don't believe that's a good idea."

Kathy sat shaking her head.

"Well *I* like the idea!" Abby exclaimed.

Gail and Brad shook hands with Jim and Kathy at the door. Gail turned toward Abby, but she drew back. She rewarded only Brad with a smile as he stopped in front of her.

"If you can think of something special you'd like for your party, let me know. I'll see what I can do. Okay?"

"Do you really mean it?"

"I really mean it!"

As they headed home Brad talked on and on, making plans. Gail sat beside him quiet and numbed.

At last she put a hand on his arm. "I want you to call them as soon as we get home. I want you to cancel the party."

"How do you tell a kid you've changed your mind and can't give her the birthday party you promised?"

Gail sighed. "I don't know." She leaned her head against the back rest. "Maybe you're right. Maybe you can't call it off."

He glanced at her. "I was wrong again?"

"This could become a disaster. Abby doesn't trust my motives. I can't say I blame her. And what about Mom and the boys? They'll expect to be included."

"Of course. They should be."

"You're moving way too fast, honey. I don't imagine Jim can afford such a celebration. Think how he must feel. As far as that goes, I'm not sure *we* can afford it."

"It's something I want to do. For you."

"For me? Or yourself? And if for yourself, why?"

They rode in silence until Gail smiled. "You know, seeing Abby today, knowing I chose to carry her rather than have an abortion, makes me feel a lot better about myself. Everything I went through to have her was worth it. Even though I was wrong to get pregnant. If I'd been a Christian then, it probably wouldn't have happened."

She saw Brad's jaw muscle tense. "What's the matter?"

"First you chew me out for finding Abby, then for offering her a party. Now you sit there congratulating yourself."

She laughed as the strain of the morning began to lift. But when she looked at Brad again she saw he really was upset.

# 8

## General Knowledge

Brad remained silent during the drive home, leaving Gail to her own thoughts. When they stopped to pick Grant and Jimmy up, Beverly excitedly questioned them. What did Abigail look like? How had she responded to Gail? Would they ever get to see her?

"The boys asked us to go to church tomorrow," Beverly mentioned, as she and Tom followed Gail and her family to the car. "I told them we just might do that. The people we met at the Christmas program certainly seemed nice."

Gail turned to her mother. "We'd love to have you."

"I know you go early for Sunday school. I thought maybe we could meet before church so we could sit together. If that's all right?"

"You're welcome to come to Sunday school with us."

"We're hardly Sunday school material," Beverly smiled. "We'll be doing good to get to church."

Later that night, after Gail had heard the boys' prayers, Jimmy poked her. "You like Grandma now, don't you, Mom?"

Gail smiled, "I'm getting to know her better. And yes, I guess I do like her."

"She told us she *loves* you," he related. "Lots!"

Grant raised himself on an elbow. "Did you and Abigail like each other?"

"We told you her name is Abby. Remember?"

"But did you like each other?" Grant persisted.

"I'm not sure how she felt. This was the first time she'd seen me. It was hard for us both."

"Kinda like with you and Grandma, huh?" Grant asked, staring at his mother. "Maybe Abby will like you better, too, when she gets to know you."

"Do you think Abby'll like us?" Jimmy questioned.

Pulling the blankets around his shoulders, Gail exclaimed, "How could she *not* like you!"

Gail was emotionally exhausted as she dragged herself off to bed. She was surprised the next morning to find she had actually slept well. Brad was quiet. He remained distant as they got ready for church.

Later that morning, when they picked the boys up at their Sunday school rooms, Jimmy announced, "I told my teacher Grant and me had a sister."

"You really shouldn't be telling people about Abby," Gail admonished.

"Why not?" Grant questioned.

Brad guided Gail by the elbow as they walked toward the church entrance. "You can't be sure the party will end all contact with her. She might even be able to spend some time with us. Get to know us and the boys. It would give Beverly a chance to meet her only granddaughter."

Spying Beverly and Tom waiting for them by the

door, the boys raced off. But Gail stopped short. "We're *not* going to do that, Brad. Abby has her life. We have ours."

"Abby's your daughter, Gail. You can't just turn your back on her."

She glared at him, pulling her arm from his grasp. "I will *not* interfere in her life. Nor will you!"

She sat sandwiched between Brad and her mother after the boys went off to childrens' church. It was impossible to concentrate on the sermon. She tried to pray. But her mind kept sprinting from one thing to another. Beverly, however, seemed intent on Pastor Martin's message.

As they were leaving Tom offered to take them all out to dinner, but Gail begged off. She was tired and wanted to go home. Although Brad was visibly upset with her, Tom appeared to understand. On the way home Brad berated her for being so cold toward her mother and Tom.

As they walked in the house Brad sent the boys off to change clothes. Then he turned on her. "Gail, what is *wrong* with you! You barely spoke to your mother and Tom."

"There's a lot on my mind. They understand. You should too—you're responsible for a good part of it."

"I suppose you're stewing over the birthday party."

"We've got to get out of that."

Brad's face blanched. "I'm fed up with your attitude, Gail."

"*My* attitude! I'm going to our room and lie down. Open some soup or something for yourself and the boys."

She was lying on the bed when she heard Brad's car pull out a few minutes later. She looked out as he drove off with Grant and Jimmy. In the kitchen was a note. They had gone to a restaurant.

Gail brooded alone in the silence of the empty house. Her feelings were jumbled. Or was it *lack* of feeling that was bothering her? Abby was Jim and Kathy's daughter; she and Abby were strangers. *Yet shouldn't I*, Gail admonished herself, *feel more of a bond to her than I do?*

The following Saturday morning Gail donned a pair of ratty jeans and an old shirt to clean house while Brad took the boys grocery shopping. They had just left when Pastor Martin called to ask if he could stop by.

When she opened the door ten minutes later, he informed her, "It seems one of the boys said something about his half sister during Sunday school. A couple of youngsters carried the tale home. People are naturally curious, Gail. Don't you think it might be a good idea to bring it out in the open? I'm sure you'll find our people ready to stand behind you when they learn what happened."

"I used to feel so ashamed. But I think I'm pretty well over that now," she smiled. "Just seeing Abby last week, remembering how Steve's mother tried to pressure me into having an abortion, made me realize I made the right choice. I wasn't a Christian back then. Other girls were having abortions. But I loved my baby from the minute I knew I was pregnant."

Gail's voice trailed away as she recalled her strong sense of protection for the unborn child she carried while little more than a child herself.

"I've been tearing myself apart all week, wondering why I didn't—*couldn't*—feel closer to Abby when I saw her. I remember having such strong nurturing feelings before she was born."

Gail stopped short, staring at Pastor Martin. "You

know, when I released Abby to the Marshals I completely let go. Just like someday, when Grant and Jimmy are grown, I'm going to have to let them go. Could that be why I feel so comfortable leaving things as they are? Leaving Abby where *she* is?"

Pastor Martin nodded. "I imagine so, Gail. Even though you weren't a Christian at the time it seems the Lord granted you both the will to make the right choices and strength to survive the outcome. Living with a Christian foster family no doubt helped."

She nodded. "It did. By the way, has Brad ever mentioned Abby to you?"

Pastor Martin shook his head. "Not a word. I've tried leaving an opening for him. But he's never taken the bait."

"He's moody again. He was more like the old Brad before we saw Abby. He was great while we were with the Marshals. Then on the way home he closed me out again. I wish I knew what was going on with him."

"I really think it might be a good idea for the two of you to come for counseling."

"He won't hear of it. I'm at a loss to know what to do. Not only about Brad, but how to stop him from going ahead with a promise he made to Abby."

She told Pastor Martin of Brad's plans for the girl's fifteenth birthday. "It would be hard to get out of now," she said as they walked to his car.

The tall man turned, placing a hand on her shoulder. "Try to get Brad to talk to me. Come together. Tell him *you* want to come and need his support."

"That would be no lie!"

He got into the car and was about to close the door when Gail stopped him. "I think you're right—it's time to let the people at church know about Abby. I value their prayers."

"Do you want me to tell them?"

She shook her head. "No. I'd like to. How about tomorrow night? After Sunday evening service."

"All right."

"Will you help me?"

Pastor Martin smiled. "Of course. Why don't you ask Brad, too. It might make him feel more a part of things."

When Brad and the boys returned home with the groceries, Gail whispered she needed to talk to him in their room. She told him about Pastor Martin's visit and deciding to tell their church family about Abby.

Brad eyed her suspiciously. "I had a feeling Pastor knew something. What made you change your mind? Last week you were in a stew over Jimmy telling his Sunday school class."

"Pastor says the story has spread. Better they hear the truth than rumors."

"What will you tell them?"

"The truth. That I was wrong in getting pregnant, but thankful I carried my baby to term."

Brad took a step back. "I see. You plan to paint yourself as something pretty special! *You* didn't have an abortion! *You* did the right thing!"

"Brad! I'm no more special than anyone else. I won't pretend I am. Will you go with me?"

"No!"

"Are you ashamed? Of me and what I've done?"

He watched her through narrowed eyes.

"Brad, I'm sorry this is hurting you. I'm sorry I was intimate before we met. I'm sorry I got pregnant—"

"Cut it out, Gail! The poor little girl begging forgiveness doesn't cut it with me!"

"What will?"

He turned to leave.

"Brad! Please—consider going with me for counseling. If you don't want to see Pastor, we can find someone else."

For the second time in their marriage Gail felt a chill of fear as rage welled hot in Brad's eyes. He then stomped from the room.

"That does it!" she muttered to herself. "That really does it!"

There was a strained silence the rest of the evening. Even Jimmy noticed. He crawled onto Gail's lap as she tried to read the newspaper after dinner and said, "Will you and Dad like each other again someday?"

Gail glanced at Brad. He was staring stonily at the television screen. "We do like each other, honey," Gail said. Although she had to admit she felt little liking *or* love for Brad at the moment.

She got ready for bed as soon as the boys were tucked in. When she came out of the bathroom she found both Brad and his car gone. Wearily she reached for the phone to call Jenny. She was relieved he was gone, relieved to be alone for awhile.

Gail told Jenny what she planned to do the following evening at church, asking Jenny and Larry to sit with her during the service. Brad would surely refuse to go.

"Of course we'll sit with you," Jenny agreed. "If you're sure you want to go through with this."

"I'm sure. It's time I faced the past and put it in proper perspective. But Jen, I don't know how much more I can take from Brad. I'm beginning to wonder if something's wrong with him."

"Mentally?"

"Yes. Or else he's jealous of my relationship with Steve."

Brad remained home with the boys the next evening. Gail's disclosure went well. Honestly she told the congregation what had happened. She told them, too, how Brad had located Abby. She noticed tears in the eyes of several after Pastor Martin led in prayer for Gail and her family, as well as for Abby and her adoptive parents. When Gail returned to her seat Jenny hugged her.

After church people came to her, assuring Gail of their prayers. She felt such release on the drive home. Her secret was hidden no longer. The veil dividing her present life from her past had been swept aside.

She found Brad waiting in the kitchen. He seemed subdued. The boys were in bed asleep. "How did it go?" he asked.

"Good. Real good."

He went to the stove. "I put water on for that hot spiced tea you like."

She sat warily at the counter. "Sounds good."

"I was thinking while you were at church. Now that people know about Abby, why don't we invite her to stay with us while Jim and Kathy are in Mexico?"

"Brad—"

"Wait!" He held up a hand. "Hear me out. We wouldn't be trying to take her away from the Marshals. Lots of kids these days have more than one family, what with all the divorces and remarriages. Abby has no brothers or sisters expect Grant and Jimmy. She should have a chance to get to know them. It would be good for her. Good for us. Besides, she didn't seem all that thrilled about going to Mexico."

Gail was shaking her head. "No, Brad! She'd have to change schools. It wouldn't work. Besides, Jim and Kathy would never allow it. They *are* her parents!"

"And *you* are her mother."

"Kathy is her mother."

"So, you're going to turn your back on her again! What kind of mother are you, anyway?"

Slipping from the stool, Gail pulled herself erect. "I'm a mother who has done what was best for her daughter. And I'll continue doing what's best by leaving her where she is. That's what kind of mother I am!" Her fear of Brad's mood was replaced by determination to protect Abby from further trauma at any cost.

The next morning Brad left the house without breakfast. Since it was Monday and she didn't have to go to work, Gail decided to go see her mother after the boys boarded the school bus. Tom took one look at her, then made an excuse about having to go somewhere.

Gail stopped him. "I'd like you to stay. I could use a male's point of view." She told of her disclosure at church and Brad's reaction. Neither Tom nor Beverly could guess what might be causing Brad's behavior.

"I don't see how I can continue this way!" Gail confided. "It's like being married to two different men. I never know which one he's going to be. It's not doing either us or the boys any good."

"You're not thinking of leaving him, are you?" her mother questioned.

"I'm not sure about anything right now."

"Maybe you should get away by yourself for awhile," Tom suggested. "Sounds like you need time alone to think."

"I don't see how I can, what with the boys in school and my job."

"You could leave the boys with us," her mother offered. "We'll take them to school and pick them up. If

Brad wanted to he could take them home at night. Or we could keep them."

"Well, I did work for Linda a few weeks ago when she was sick. She might be willing to take my shift for the rest of the week. But—" She looked closely at her mother and Tom. "Are you sure you wouldn't mind keeping the boys?"

Tom smiled. "Wouldn't mind at all."

"Where would you go?" Beverly questioned. "What would you do?"

"I know exactly where I'll go. And if you don't mind, I'll go today. I'll bring the boys back here after school and be gone before Brad gets home."

Beverly shook her head. "Honey, don't leave without telling him. He's been a good husband. A good father. Explain you need to get away for a few days."

As Gail left the apartment she hugged her mother. "Thanks Mom. It's good having you and Tom close by."

Tears filled Beverly's eyes. "I knew you weren't looking forward to our moving here. But as I told Tom, I'd love you so much someday you'd love me back."

Tom hugged Gail, too. She looked first at one, then the other. "I guess I've finally got a mom *and* a dad."

She drove straight home to call Linda, who agreed to cover for her. She packed, then called to let Jenny know she wouldn't be taking care of the boys that week. Jenny agreed Gail probably needed to get away. But she also cautioned Gail not to leave without telling Brad.

"I'll stop by his office on my way out of town."

"Where are you going?"

"I'd rather not say. I don't want Brad trying to get it out of you."

"How long will you be gone?"

"I'm not sure. I'll probably be back before the weekend."

Gail decided to let Pastor Martin know her plans in case Brad went to him after she left. But first there was another call to make.

Kathy Marshal didn't seem surprised to hear from Gail.

"I figured Abby would be in school. I just wanted you to know I don't plan to interfere in your lives."

There was silence. Finally Kathy asked, "Then why did your husband call Jim suggesting we leave Abby with you while we go to Mexico?"

Gail couldn't believe it. "He did what?"

"We haven't told Abby. But there's no way we'd agree. I don't think she would either. Her school is here. Her friends and Cody—the boy she thinks she's in love with—are here. If she didn't have to go with us I'm sure she'd rather remain in Eaton with the family of a friend. But she *is* going with us."

"I'm sorry, Kathy. I truly am. I had no idea Brad had been in contact with you about this. He mentioned it to me last night, but I told him we could never offer such a thing. In fact, our marriage is so torn apart over it I'm thinking of leaving him."

Until then Gail hadn't admitted, even to herself, she was considering a permanent separation. "I'm going away for a few days to think things through."

"I'm sorry, Gail. I haven't stopped to consider what this might be doing to you and your family."

"How is Abby? I mean, how was she after we met?"

"It's hard to tell. Teenagers confide in friends rather than family. But Gail, Jim and I are terribly upset about this birthday party."

"That wasn't my idea. Do you think Abby would be too disappointed if we called it off?"

"Probably. She's been telling everyone."

"Has she told her friends about me?"

"Yes. I overheard her describe how pretty you are to one of her girl friends. And how young." Hurt edged Kathy's voice. "Jim and I are nearer the age of her friend's grandparents."

"I'm sorry you and Jim are hurting over this. Honest, Kathy, I'm not trying to wedge my way into Abby's life. I'd never try taking your place with her. You and Jim can rest assured of that, at least."

# 9

## *Off Alone*

The school bus moaned to a stop to let the boys off as Gail hung the phone up after talking to Kathy Marshal. There was no time now to let Pastor Martin know of her plans.

Grant and Jimmy were excited when she told them they'd be spending a few days with their grandparents. Jimmy didn't even question where his mother was going or why. Grant did—as she had expected.

"Are you and Dad mad again?"

She decided to be honest. Grant would never let her get by with anything less. "Your dad and I are having a little difference of opinion. It'll be good for us to have a short vacation from each other. But don't worry. We're going to get it all straightened out soon." *Am I being entirely honest with him? Or myself?* she wondered.

Gail pulled Grant to her. She ran a hand along the

nape of his neck. His dark eyes searched hers. "Honey, I'm praying about it. And I'm sure your father is, too. God knows and cares about us. All of us."

"I pray for you and Dad every night," the boy said. "After our out-loud prayers I add things of my own."

She hugged him. "That's good! With your prayers added to ours, we can't lose." Looking again into his face, Gail stressed, "I want you to have a good time. I'll call every afternoon as soon as you and Jimmy get home from school. Okay?"

He nodded doubtfully. "I guess—"

Gail dropped the boys off at her mother's then drove directly to the newspaper office. She made her way through the crowded news room with its clutter of desks, clicking computer keyboards, and low mutter of voices. A chill gripped her when she glanced back across the room as she reached Brad's office door. The desktop computer monitors resembled upright tombstones. Was it a premonition? Was she dealing her marriage its deathblow?

She knocked lightly on the door while pushing it open. "May I come in?"

Brad looked up.

"I called Kathy Marshal this afternoon," Gail announced, closing the door behind her. "She told me you'd talked to Jim about Abby staying with us while they're in Mexico."

"Gail, I—"

She held up a hand. "The Marshals aren't about to let Abby stay with us. Neither am I. But that's not what I came to talk about. I'm going away for a few days. Mom and Tom have agreed to keep the boys. You can pick them up in the evenings if you want. Or they can stay there all night. Mom offered to take them to school and pick them up."

Brad betrayed no emotion. He tilted back in his swivel chair. "Where are you going?" His voice was cool.

"I'd rather not say. I need time by myself. You probably do, too."

He shrugged. "Maybe."

Gail moved back toward the door. She didn't know what else to say. He seemed a stranger. "I'll call the boys every afternoon so they won't think I've deserted them."

Brad stared. At last he got to his feet. He walked to the front of the desk, leaning back against it, arms folded, head cocked to one side. "You won't tell me where you're going?"

She glanced away. "I'd rather not."

"When will you be back?"

Her determination was crumbling. She longed for him to hold her. She was tempted to throw herself in his arms. But she didn't. "I should be back by the weekend. Maybe before."

"What then?"

Gail shook her head. "I don't know. That's what I need to think through. To pray about." She opened the door. If she didn't leave she wouldn't be able to. "I hope you'll be doing the same, Brad."

"What makes you think I haven't?"

"I—I'll see you in a few days." Gail opened the door to retreat back through the news room. In the hallway she stopped to glance around. Brad was watching her from his office doorway. Their eyes met just before he turned away.

Twilight was stealing the day as Gail drove out of town—alone. She was glad it would soon be dark. People wouldn't be able to see her wiping at the tears. She gripped the steering wheel, her heart feeling like a leaden rock.

Two hours later, after eating at a truck stop cafe along the freeway, Gail reached the familiar town of her birth. She rented a room at one of the newer motels on the outskirts of town.

After unpacking, she ran the bathtub full of hot water and slipped down into its relaxing depths. She closed her eyes and leaned back, letting the tension slowly ease from her body and soul.

For the first time in years she didn't have to think of anyone but herself. She didn't have to explain what she was doing or why. She could do whatever she pleased, whenever she pleased. It seemed strange but good, even though guilt at running off from her family was tugging at her.

"I needed this time alone with you, Lord."

She thought back on the tiny studio apartment where she had lived alone in this very town before meeting Brad. The apartment had been small and plain. While she had been lonely at times, she had mostly enjoyed being on her own. She'd made friends at work. There had been Lorna, her one and only girl friend from high school. And of course, Sue and Mack Grant. And then she had met Brad—

"Brad." She spoke his name aloud. "I was so in love with you." Her words startled her, popping her eyes open. "I didn't mean *was* in love. It's just that you've been so difficult to love lately."

With her bath over Gail got into bed. She planned to read her Bible, then a novel. Instead she fell asleep, awaking two hours later. She turned off the light and lay there listening to the sounds outside. A car door slammed. Footsteps twanged up a metal stairway. A television clicked off on the opposite side of the wall. Finally a numbing sleep closed over her again.

In the morning Gail awoke in the strange bed, trying to put together the pieces of the day before. Twenty-four hours ago she had been in her own bed, with no idea she wouldn't be there this morning.

She got up and dressed before calling Sue to tell her foster mother where she was and what she had done. "How about meeting me for lunch?" Gail invited. "My treat."

Gail ate breakfast at the motel restaurant. Then she drove slowly around town, looking at familiar and new sights. The old apartment building where she had lived after leaving the Grants was shabbier than before. But the office complex where she had worked looked refurbished.

The church she had attended with the Grants was no different. There was a new minister there, according to the sign. The high school was bigger. The huge old maple trees lining the street she had walked to and from school had been trimmed.

She pulled her car to the curb. She was at the corner where she had waited for Steve after school to tell him, that fateful fall day fifteen years ago, that she was pregnant with his baby.

A chilly January wind slammed against the car as she sat there remembering—her memories as raw and biting as the wind. She had longed for Steve to hold her back then, yearned for him to take care of her and their baby.

But he had turned away. The hopelessness she had felt then surged over her again. It reminded her of yesterday and Brad's seeming indifference.

At last she started the car. On her way downtown to meet Sue, Gail couldn't resist driving past the house where Steve, Abby's father, had lived with his parents. It looked smaller.

Gail smiled. "Lord, that house seemed positively huge when Steve brought me here the first time. The time his mother tried talking me into an abortion."

When Gail walked into the restaurant where she was to meet Sue, she found the woman waiting by the cash register. They followed the waitress to a booth by a window overlooking the street.

After ordering Sue asked, "So what's this about, Gail?"

"I needed time alone to think things through. I didn't want to have to explain to the boys why I wasn't smiling, or why Brad and I had argued the night before. Grant and Jimmy needed time away from the tension, too."

"Has it been that bad?"

Gail nodded. "It's been building for weeks." She told Sue about Brad locating Abby, and of meeting with the girl and her parents. "I can't take much more. Brad blows hot, then cold. He's changed during the last few months. There've been times I've actually been afraid of him."

"Has he hit you?"

"No. But he came close once."

The waitress brought coffee. Gail waited until she left, staring down into her cup. "I know I haven't been easy to live with lately. I've been obsessed with memories as Abby's fifteenth birthday gets closer. Memories of when I was her age. I talked to our pastor about it.

"For awhile it seemed Brad and I were getting things squared away. Then he found Abby. Sue, overnight Brad went from refusing to talk about my daughter, to acting as though she was *his* child."

"What do you plan to do now?" Sue asked. "Do you really think your leaving will accomplish anything?"

"I only know I had to get out of there for awhile. By the way, do you know if Lorna still lives in town? I haven't seen her since Brad and I got married."

"I ran into her at the grocery store the other day. She has four youngsters and another on the way. She asked about you."

"I've forgotten her married name."

"Thompson. Her husband's first name is Joe. She talks about him all the time."

"I drove past Steve's parents' house. It looks the same, only not nearly as impressive." She sighed. "I wonder if Steve has told his wife about our daughter? Do you suppose he ever thinks of his first child?"

"I imagine he's been thinking about her a lot, now that he and his wife have a daughter of their own."

A clatter of dishes came from the kitchen. Gail gazed wistfully out at the street as a car passed. The gray sky was promising snow. "I'd like to tell Steve about seeing Abby."

"Gail, please don't contact Steve after all this time!"

The waitress brought their seafood salads and they began to eat.

"Why don't you come stay with us?" Sue suggested. "Your old room isn't being used."

"There are too many memories there. But thanks anyway."

"Come for dinner tomorrow night, then?"

Gail smiled. "Thanks. I'd like that."

Gail drove back to her motel after leaving the restaurant. It seemed voicing a desire to contact Steve had chiseled the longing into her mind. Memories and feelings were seeping in. They brought to life again her nearly forgotten yearnings for Steve to rescue her after she found she carried their child.

She came to despise him for abandoning her and their baby. As time went on she entered the Salvation Army home to await their child's birth. Then, while in the hospital shortly before Abby was born, Steve had unexpectedly showed up. He told her of his grief and hurt over what was happening. Until then, she had had no idea it was bothering him.

She reached for the phone book to look up his parent's number. She hadn't spoken to Joanna Miller since before Abby was born. She doubted Steve's mother would recognize her voice. She could truthfully tell the woman she was a former classmate of Steve's. Joanna might give her Steve's address.

No! She couldn't do that. Pushing the temptation from her, Gail flipped the pages on to the Thompsons. She came to a Joe Thompson, and under that a Joseph Thompson. She dialed the first number.

The receiver was picked up on the fourth ring. "Hello?"

"I'd like to speak to Lorna Thompson, please."

"This is Lorna."

"Lorna! This is Gail. Gail Richards. Or at least it used to be Richards before it became Lorring."

"Gail?" Lorna squealed. "I was thinking about you just the other day. I thought about trying to get your address from Mrs. Grant."

Lorna prattled on and on about "her Joe" and the four little Thompsons.

"I remember you always wanted a big family," Gail noted. "Sounds as though you're happy."

"Well, most of the time. Sometimes the kids get to be a bit much. I'm not going to have any more after this fifth one. Joe says we can't afford anymore on his salary. I've been doing day care to help out."

Lorna invited Gail to come over later that evening

to meet Joe and the kids. "I'd ask you to come for dinner, but I don't think you'd enjoy it much. It can get pretty hectic here at mealtime."

Next Gail dialed her mother's number and talked to Grant and Jimmy for a few minutes. It sounded as though they were having a good time. Her mother told her Brad had picked the boys up the night before and dropped them off that morning.

Gail ate dinner alone in the motel restaurant, then drove to the opposite side of town searching for the address Lorna had given her. She found an obviously pregnant, overweight Lorna in a small cluttered house. Slight, dark-haired Joe was helping his wife clear the dishes. Two small boys and a couple of slightly older girls shyly watched Gail.

Joe finally herded them off to the living room, leaving Gail and Lorna alone in the hall-like kitchen. Gail dried the dishes as Lorna washed, while rambling on about Joe, with whom she was obviously in love.

Depression groped for and found Gail as she drove back to the motel. She was glad Lorna was happy. But sad and guilt-stricken that she herself was not. Materially she had so much more than her former schoolmate. And here she was running from it. If only Brad hadn't changed so!

Her thoughts turned back to Steve again. If she called and Steve's mother recognized her voice, the woman would never give her Steve's address. Maybe she could send him a letter at his parent's home. She'd write "please forward" on the envelope. They'd never know who it was from if she didn't include her return address. *No! If the letter was forwarded to Steve's home, his wife might get hold of it*, she thought.

"Lord," Gail called out, "my better judgment tells

me not to do this. Yet I want to."

She ran the bathtub full again, taking another long hot soak. She tried to pray as she lay back in the tub. But she couldn't rid her mind of the longing to talk to Steve. *Why do I think he would or could do anything to console me after all this time?* she wondered. *He didn't help me before. Besides, he's married now. And so am I!*

Gail stepped from the tub to wrap herself in the new, rose-colored Christmas robe Brad and the boys had given her, vigorously brushing at her hair. In midstroke she dropped the brush on the bedstand and reached for the phone. Her fingers were closing over the receiver to dial the Millers' number when the phone rang under her hand. She jerked back before reaching for the receiver again.

"Hello?"

"So—you are there."

Gail froze. "Brad! How did you know?"

"I figured you'd go to the Grants. I called and talked Sue into telling me where you were."

She swallowed down her shock, then asked, "Is everything all right? I talked to the boys a little while ago."

"I left them at your mother's tonight." He was silent for a moment, then added, "I miss you, Gail. The house is so quiet with you and the kids gone. It feels like someone died."

Warmth flooded her. "I thought you might enjoy the quiet after the arguments we've been having."

"No matter what our differences, Gail, I'm not complete without you."

Guiltily Gail thought of her yearnings for Steve. She had been so hurt and angry with Brad it had blocked her feelings for him. Now they all flooded back. "I had to get away. But I must admit it hasn't done a whole lot of good." She told him then about seeing Sue and visiting Lorna.

Although nothing was resolved between them, Gail felt better when they hung up. She had promised to be home when he got off work the next day. He suggested she leave the boys with Beverly and Tom so they could go out to dinner and talk before taking Grant and Jimmy back home with them.

She was thankful she hadn't called the Millers, positive it was the Lord who had stopped her. God had no doubt prompted Brad to call just then. "Thank you, Lord," she breathed as she slipped off to sleep.

Gail was packing her suitcase the next morning when she remembered Sue had invited her for dinner that night. She called her foster mother, telling her she was going home instead.

"Good. I'm glad. That's where you belong. Keep in touch. I'll be praying for you."

She took to the side roads on the way back to Linden, enjoying the winter day while enclosed within the warmth of the car. She lingered over a sandwich and cup of tea at a cafe, content to be going home. She felt relief and peace as she realized how narrowly she had escaped the temptation to get in touch with Steve. It was Brad she had needed all the time.

The sky was spitting snow by the time she turned into her driveway. She called her mother to let her know she was home but wouldn't come for the boys until after dinner. Gail unpacked and slipped into Brad's favorite blue dress for their dinner date.

She picked up her Bible as she pulled a chair close to the living room window so she could watch the snowflakes. She opened the Bible to the book of

Psalms. She needed all the guidance she could get, all the Lord could muster within her, as she and Brad tried to set their marriage on a smoother course.

She met Brad later at the back door. Wordlessly she went into his arms. They held each other for several long moments before she pulled back. "I do love you, Brad."

"I realize I haven't been easy to love lately. But, Gail, I love you too."

"My past is to blame. We've been going through such a tough time trying to deal with it all."

Sucking in an edge-sharp breath, Brad glanced away. "I haven't been so perfect myself."

Gail reached up to stroke his cheek. "No one's perfect. Not even Christians. It comforts me to know I wasn't a Christian when I got pregnant. I know the Lord has forgiven me. It's just that it's so hard living with the consequences."

She smiled sadly. "We're both having to live with those consequences."

"I admit the thought of you being with someone else before me, sharing a baby with him, chews me up sometimes. But I'm trying, Gail. I really am."

So! There it was at last! Gail kissed him on the cheek. "I'm sorry, honey. But there's nothing I can do to change the past."

"Be patient with me, Gail. We'll work it out. *I'll* work it out."

"We need help, Brad. Won't you go for counseling with me?"

"No!" He stepped back from her. "We have the Lord. That should be enough!"

# 10

## A Plea for Help

The atmosphere during dinner at the small Italian restaurant grew strained with Brad and Gail avoiding all subjects that could cause conflict. They lingered at the table after dessert, reluctant to leave their demilitarized zones, yet finding little to say.

Gail finally tried to bury one bone of contention by talking Brad into agreeing never to contact the Marshals again without checking with her. That brought her a measure of peace.

Saturday Gail felt a stab of loss when she realized this was the day Abby and her parents were to leave for Mexico. They'd be gone three months. What of the party when they returned? Could she and Brad somehow get out of it without hurting Abby?

Beverly and Tom attended church with them from time to time during the following weeks. One evening Jimmy announced, "Grandma listened to our prayers when you was away, and we stayed with her and Grandpa."

Patting him on the head, Gail remarked absently, "That's nice, honey." At least her mother was making an effort to carry out the lifestyle they had established for their family.

Life slowly settled back to near normal. Gail and Jenny helped with the women's annual winter dinner at church. Beverly attended the evening event with Gail, seeming to enjoy herself. It was actually good having her mother and Tom close by, she decided.

Gail was again bringing clothing home from the Crisis Pregnancy Center to wash and iron. And she was regularly donating some of her own money to the cause. But when Mrs. Philips asked her to help with the Hot Line, Gail turned her down. Brad seemed to be having no problem talking about Abby now. But for some strange reason mention of the center continued to irritate him.

By mid-March birds returned to establish nesting rights. Daffodils speared their way through the soil of Gail's flower bed bordering the driveway. The days grew longer as the earth tilted them back toward the warmth of spring and summer.

One particularly warm, fragrant evening Brad came home from work wearing a canary-swallowing grin. In his hand was a letter. He held it out to Gail. "This came to the office today. Look at the postmark."

She was in their bedroom changing clothes after work. Gail took the envelope and turned it over. "Mexico? From Jim?"

"No. Abby. Look how it's addressed." He pointed to the neat handwriting on the front. "It was sent to me in care of The Linden Newspaper. It seems we have a smart girl."

There was that *we* again. "Why did she write to you? Is she all right?"

He nodded. "Read it."

Gail dropped weakly to the edge of the bed. She pulled the single folded sheet of paper from its small white envelope. She had never seen her daughter's handwriting before.

> Dear Mr. Lorring,
> Mexico is okay. But I'll sure be glad to get home. We have another three weeks left here. I hope it goes by fast.
> Did you mean it when you offered to give me a birthday party at a restaurant? My dad won't talk to me about it. Mom says you were probably just making conversation. Were you?
> I don't think your wife liked the idea much. So maybe by now, if you did mean it, she's talked you out of the party. If she has, I'll understand and know it wasn't your fault.
> Please don't let my folks know I've written. If Mrs. Lorring finds out, ask her not to say anything to them. It would be better if you didn't try to answer this letter, I guess. If you weren't just making conversation, about the party I mean, you can get in touch with us when we get back home.
> Soon to be fifteen,
> Abby

Gail refolded the letter and slipped it back in its envelope. Abby's reference to her hurt. *Your wife*, she had written, evidently unwilling to acknowledge her as anything more than Brad's wife. It was a slap in the face, whether intentional or not. "Well, *you* seem to have made a hit with her."

"Aren't you excited? That she wrote us, I mean?"

"Excited about what? She wrote to you, not me. Doesn't it bother you she seems interested only in the party? In what she can get out of you?"

"It could grow into a beginning between her and us."

"Between her and *you*," Gail corrected.

Brad's eyes narrowed. He looked down at Gail. "Now who's showing signs of jealously?"

"Brad, why are you so taken with this girl?" Gail inquired as she pulled on jeans and a peach-colored blouse.

"This *girl*, as you put it, is your daughter."

"I don't understand why you insist we get involved with her. This is the very same girl you refused to talk about until a few weeks ago." She paused at the bedroom door before heading for the kitchen to start dinner. "Why, Brad?"

He shook his head. "I don't know. I can't say."

"Can't? Or won't?" she tossed back as she pulled the door shut.

After dinner, with the boys asleep and Brad watching television, Gail sat down on the couch by him. "Honey, I really wish you'd cancel Abby's party."

"I don't see how I can."

"The Marshal's may simply refuse to come. Or to let Abby come."

"She's a strong-willed kid," Brad replied. "They won't be able to refuse without causing themselves grief."

Surprised at the satisfied ring to his voice, Gail frowned. "You really want to go through with this, don't you?"

He nodded. "It could edge us into Abby's life."

"I don't want to intrude in her life. She has a good life without us. Her parents love her; I'm sure she loves them. She knows how to get in touch with us if she ever wants to. But for now—"

"Gail, this is a chance to have a small part in our—*your*—daughter's life. You've lost the first fifteen years. You shouldn't have to give up anymore."

"But honey, real love is giving. Not manipulating to get something for yourself. When a person holds on too tight they choke the life out of those they love. I don't want to do that to Abby any more than to our sons. If I interfere in her growing up now, that's exactly what I'll be doing."

Brad stood. "I don't see how we can get out of the party. I've already reserved a small room at The Towers. If you aren't interested in helping I'll find someone who is."

The next day Gail called Pastor Martin during her break at work. She told him about Abby's letter and of Brad's determination to go ahead with the party. "Could you please talk to him?"

Saturday morning Pastor Martin called Brad to ask if he could come to the church for a few minutes. "Probably needs help moving something," Brad commented as he left. "He's been talking about changing the church office around."

But when Brad returned an hour later he was smoldering. "Can't keep anything to yourself, can you?"

"Not when I see you disrupting the Marshals' lives," Gail told him calmly. "Did Pastor Martin get through to you?"

"Oh, he got through! But it won't change a thing."

When Gail learned her mother was helping Brad with the party, she confronted Beverly. "Why are you doing this? Pastor Martin, Jenny, Sue, the Marshals—everyone who knows what Brad's doing feels it's wrong."

"Abby's my granddaughter. Brad's only trying to bring us together."

"I know what Brad's trying to do. What I don't know is why."

"Let it be, Gail. When we first moved here you were

skeptical about having me around the boys. But that has worked out all right. Maybe this will, too."

The days blurred from one to another, with nothing resolved. Then one Monday morning Gail answered the telephone while cooking breakfast for Grant and Jimmy. It was an obviously upset Kathy Marshal. Gail asked if she'd mind calling back after the boys left for school, then waited on edge for the phone to ring again after they were gone.

At last it shrilled with Gail nearly dropping the receiver in her rush to pick it up. "Hello?"

"I'm sorry to have called too early before. Abby had already left for school. I figured you're boys probably had, too."

"When did you get back from Mexico?"

"A few days ago. Since then our problems with Abby have escalated."

"Is it because of the party Brad's planning?"

There was a long silence. Kathy sighed. "You mean he's actually going ahead? I thought maybe he'd changed his mind. Or that you had talked him out of it."

"I've tried. He won't budge. He says—and I suppose he has a point—that if he doesn't go through with it now, Abby'll feel I've abandoned her again."

"You didn't abandon her. You made it possible for her to have a home and family."

"I know. That's how I look at it. But Brad sees it differently."

"Well, that's something we'll have to face later. There's a more pressing problem right now. It's Abby's boy friend. He moved here from another state with his father a few months ago. At first Abby felt sorry for him. His parents had split up, with his mother keeping his two sisters. It seems she didn't want Cody.

*112*

"We wouldn't let Abby date the boy, but encouraged her to invite him to our home and to church. Jim and I tried our best to help him. To befriend him. He went to church with us at first. But I could see it was only to please our daughter. He ridiculed God, Jim's sermons, everything we hold dear."

"How does Abby feel about that?" Gail questioned.

"I'm afraid he's managed to turn things around. Instead of Abby influencing Cody for the Lord, the boy has her questioning our beliefs and values. To tell you the truth, I'm frightened. She's so young and inexperienced. What if she should—what I mean is, I'm fearful she may lower her moral standards. We don't allow her to date yet, but she still sees this boy at school. We can't watch her every minute."

"You're worried she might become sexually active?"

"It has crossed our minds more than once."

There it was! The very fear that had been plaguing Gail. "I'm sure you've raised Abby to know the Lord."

"When she was younger her love for Jesus was beautiful. Now—well, I'm afraid she's leaning toward the lifestyle of her more radical school friends."

"So this rebellion she's into started before we met. I was afraid I was the cause. I could tell she wasn't thrilled to see me."

"Yes, it started before that. But I must admit it has worsened since. Don't misunderstand. I'm not blaming you, Gail. In fact, I'm coming to you, counting on your help."

"Me?" How could she help? Especially after Abby's reaction to her. And then there was that letter—the one Abby had sent to Brad that snubbed her. "The only thing I can think of would be for me to fade completely out of your lives."

"It's too late, Gail. I'd like you to talk to her. I'll arrange it so Abby's here alone. If you could come to the house she'll have to stay put and listen."

"What could I possibly say to her?"

"You must have had a rough time when you were her age and found yourself pregnant. All those months carrying your baby, only to give her up. Maybe you could tell her what it was like. Apparently you thought you had a good relationship with Abby's father before you became pregnant. Yet it appears you had to face her birth and loss alone."

"I did. But I'm not sure telling Abby would help. What about your husband? How does he feel?"

"I haven't told him. I thought it might be best if our husbands didn't know until afterward. Jim would probably try to stop us. And I have a feeling your husband would insist on coming. If you aren't alone with Abby you won't be able to say what needs to be said. I'd like it to be just you and her."

Kathy asked Gail to call her the following morning with a decision. "Please," Kathy begged, "try to see your way clear to do this. For Abby. For all of us."

Gail sat in the quiet of her home for a long time after hanging up. Outside a dog barked. A car horn sounded on the street. Then it was quiet again. Gail's body remained motionless while her mind raced. At last she picked up the phone and dialed the church, only to get an answering machine. She had forgotten it was Monday, Pastor Martin's day off. An emergency number was on the recorder. But this wasn't an emergency. Or was it?

How could she not try to help her daughter? Gail recalled her own teenage desperation, and her earlier childhood. She hadn't been blessed with loving parents as Abby enjoyed. Her own mother had been impregnated by one of the men—Beverly never knew which—she brought home after her late night shift at the lounge.

Beverly's husband at the time had been away, working in Alaska. He divorced Beverly when the months of her baby's delivery didn't add up to nine. Twelve years later the authorities took Gail from her alcoholic mother. Vaguely she recalled the succession of foster homes that ended two years later at the Grants.

Gail remembered not getting along at first with Ginger, Sue and Mack's daughter. Then she had met Steve. Tall blond Steve Miller, son of a prominent doctor, who planned also to be a doctor. Steve, who at seventeen was two years older and could have dated any girl, had chosen her! At least she thought he had.

She closed her eyes as the memories washed over her in sickening waves.

Then she had found herself pregnant. Gail at first fantasized her relationship with Steve would become permanent. They'd marry and always be together, loving one another and their baby. She'd at last have a home of her own. A family. But Steve had turned away, leaving her to decide alone what to do with the tiny, helpless life growing inside her.

Now, it appeared, Abby might well find herself on a similar detour. "Lord, what should I do? Should I see Abby? Try talking to her?"

Gail dreaded seeing Abby alone, telling the girl about her past. But she couldn't live with herself, she admitted, if she didn't at least try talking to her daughter. With dread she dialed the Marshal's.

Kathy's voice revealed her relief at hearing from Gail so soon. "Thank you. When can you come?"

"How about tomorrow?"

Kathy gave her their address and directions. She

would see to it Abby was alone at four when she returned from school.

Gail didn't want her mother to know what she was about to do, and so she called Jenny to ask if she could leave the boys with her after school. Jenny agreed. Gail then told her what she was about to do.

"Why don't I keep the boys until after dinner," Jenny offered. "That way you'll be free to tell Brad what happened after you get home."

"Thanks, Jen. Please pray for me. I have no idea what I'm going to say to Abby or to Brad afterward."

Gail ended the conversation, then slipped to her knees in the quiet house. "Lord, guide me. Give me strength to say the right things to Abby. Hold onto her so she won't slip away, Lord. If I can't count on you, there's no one left to count on."

# 11

## Confrontation

Gail prayed the miles away on her drive to Eaton the following afternoon. She had stopped by the church to talk with Pastor Martin. He prayed with her, then asked permission to alert a few church members to pray while she was talking to Abby.

It was ten minutes after four when Gail stopped in front of the white, two-story house bearing the address Kathy Marshal had given her. It was old but well-maintained, with a wide front porch perfect for sipping lemonade on warm summer evenings.

Briefly Gail closed her eyes. "Lord, help me." She opened the car door and walked with wooden legs to the porch and up the steps. She pressed the bell by the solid front door. Chimes rang. A thundering of footfalls followed as someone rushed downstairs.

The door flew open. "I told you to come to the back in case my folks—" Abby stopped, staring at Gail. "Oh! It's you! I thought—what are *you* doing here?"

Gail tried to smile. "I came to see you."

Abby partially closed the door. "I don't think my folks would want you here."

"Your mother asked me to come."

"She did? Why?"

"I'll tell you if you let me come inside."

"Well—" The girl hesitated, then opened the door wider. Behind her a narrow stairway hugged one wall of a hall leading toward the back of the house. A barefoot Abby wore jeans and a pink tank top that did nothing to hide her well-developed figure. She went into the living room and flopped onto an over-stuffed chair.

Taking a vague hand movement toward the other chairs as an invitation to sit down, Gail chose an afghan-covered wooden rocker near the girl. "Your mother called yesterday. It surprised me as much as my coming today surprised you."

Gail wondered what to say next. *Lord!* she called out in silent desperation. *Help me! Listen to those praying for me back home at this very moment.*

"I'll bet Dad doesn't know Mom called you. He thinks you're trying to push your way into our lives."

"I could tell you weren't overjoyed the day we met. I didn't know Brad was trying to find you or had set that meeting up until it was done."

"I remember you said that. You didn't want me when I was born. And you didn't want to see me after I'd grown up."

Gail leaned forward. "It wasn't like that. I just didn't want to upset your lives."

"Why are you here now, then?"

"Because, as I said, your mother—your adoptive mother I mean—asked me to come talk to you."

"You mean my *real* mother. You're only my birth

mother. And as far as I'm concerned, that doesn't count for a lot."

Anger hammered in Gail's temples. Her first impulse was to defend herself, to point out that if she hadn't continued the pregnancy, abortion would have flushed Abby away. But again she held her peace.

"Your mother thought you should know what happened to me before you were born."

The girl stretched her arms above her head, smiling impishly as though bored by the conversation. "I know how babies are made."

"And how they're aborted?" Gail asked, anger rising closer to the surface, along with an instinctive desire for self-vindication.

"I know all about it. Now you'll tell how you might have aborted me. But you loved me too much. Since I already know that stuff, what else is there to say?"

Gail concentrated on allowing the tension to drain from her. "I think you should know what got me into that situation."

Abby shrugged, commenting in a bored tone, "Go ahead, if you must."

"I didn't have a good home life, Abby, the way you seem to have here," Gail began. She told about her mother and about the man she thought was her father until she was fifteen and pregnant.

She sensed Abby's boredom lessening. "When I found I was carrying a baby, I resolved you'd have an easier time of it. I gave you up not because I didn't want or love you, but because I wanted you to have something I'd never had."

Abby's belligerence faded as she noted, "Looking at you is kind of spooky. You know? It's like seeing what I'll look like when I'm older."

Then she asked, "What was my natural father like?"

Gail drew in her breath. How could she explain Steve to their daughter? "He was good looking. A senior when I was a sophomore. The son of a doctor. I'd never dated before Steve—that was his name. I thought he loved me. After he found you were on the way, I hated him for turning away from me.

"Then, shortly before you were born, I nearly had a miscarriage. He heard about it and came to the hospital. He had been planning to go to college and prepare to become a doctor like his father. But as time went on, he told me he couldn't bring himself to just walk away from us. He admitted he didn't love me. Yet he offered marriage so I could keep you. But I knew it wouldn't work. By then I realized I wasn't in love with him. He left town for awhile right after graduating from high school."

"Where is he now?" Abby questioned. "What became of him?"

"He *is* a doctor. He and his wife live somewhere on the East Coast."

Abby slouched thoughtfully, pulling her feet up under her. "Does he know you've found me?"

Gail shook her head. "I haven't talked to Steve since that day in the hospital before you were born. I don't know if he ever told his wife about you, in case you're thinking of trying to get in touch with him."

"I might like to. Someday."

So, Gail thought, hurt rising to nearly choke her. Abby might be interested in finding her birth father. But she wanted nothing to do with her birth mother. "I don't think it would be a good idea."

The girl's eyes narrowed. "Well, I didn't think meeting *you* was a good idea, either!"

An uncomfortable silence hung over the room. Abby brooded as Gail tried to pull herself back on track, back to the reason she had come.

"Your parents are worried about you, Abby. So am I. We don't want you slipping into the same trap I got myself into when I was your age."

"I suppose Mom told you about Cody."

"She said he was alienating you from them and from God."

"Cody's been through a lot. His mother took his younger sisters when she left him and his dad. At first I just wanted to be his friend. Then I found I loved him."

"Do you love him—or feel sorry for him?"

Abby shrugged. "Both I guess."

"Your mother told me he continually jabs at God and the church. Everything your family believes in."

"He doesn't understand. He will."

"And if he doesn't? If he never accepts your faith?"

"I'll love him anyway," Abby declared.

"When did he first try to persuade you to become intimate?"

The girl's face flushed. "What makes you think —he'd never leave me, at least. Not the way my father left you!"

Gail recalled a similar declaration she had made about Steve. "Abby, it sounds as though you're in way over your head with this boy."

"Just like you, huh? You *can* be careful, you know. You don't *have* to get pregnant. My friends just look on it as a way of showing how much you care about each other."

"I used to think that myself," Gail admitted. "Even after I found I was pregnant. Then I learned the way God looks on sex for people not married to one another. It's wrong, Abby. It's not what God wants for us. It hurts our bodies and our spirits. It hurts those we eventually marry. God just didn't build us to handle the powerful things sex does to us outside of marriage."

"Well, for your information, Cody and I haven't done anything." A twisted smile blushed her face. "Not yet, anyway."

"What if he insists? What then?"

"Why should it matter to you? You're not responsible for me."

"No, but I care about you. So do your parents. And, Abby, so does God."

The girl's eyes wandered away. "I love Cody and he loves me. If a baby came before we got married, Cody would stand by me."

"So—he *has* pressured you."

The girl's face shaded to a deeper pink. "Like Cody says, if we weren't meant to do it, God wouldn't have put so much 'want to' in us."

Gail slipped from the rocker to the floor in front of the girl, putting her hands on Abby's knees. "God is able to help you control even the wants. Give God a chance. Believe me, sex at your age isn't worth the consequences."

"I'm the consequence of what you and my father did. You're saying I'm not worth it?"

"You're twisting my words."

Gail reached out to the girl, but Abby drew back. She got to her feet. "I think you'd better go before Dad comes home. He won't like it when he finds Mom asked you to come here."

At the front door Gail turned back. "I love you, Abby."

She was on the porch when the girl finally spoke. "I suppose you expect me to give Cody up just because you've made the supreme effort to tell me I should."

"At least think about what I've said. Neither your parents nor I want to see you hurt. We love you."

"And I love Cody!"

Tears blurred Gail's vision as she walked to the car. She had failed.

"Mrs. Lorring?" Abby was walking across the lawn toward her. "Will there still be a party for my birthday? Or has your husband changed his mind?"

"You'll have to talk to him about that. I personally feel it's a mistake."

The girl's steel seemed to be disintegrating. "You tell me you care about me. Yet my birthday means nothing to you." Tears erupted. Furiously she brushed at them, instantly hostile again. "You don't care about me. Not like my adoptive parents and Cody."

Grief got into the car with Gail. She watched as Abby ran barefoot back to the house before turning the ignition key.

"Lord," Gail prayed as she pulled onto the freeway bound for home, "Abby has no idea how much her birthday means to me. Maybe Brad's right. Maybe we do have to go ahead with the party."

Brad's car was in the driveway when Gail reached home. He was standing in the open doorway as she walked to the house. "So you broke down and went to see Abby," he remarked with evident satisfaction.

"How did you know?" She entered the kitchen, closing the door behind her. "I left the boys at Jen's so we could talk."

Brad looked more than a bit pleased with himself. "Abby called me at work after you left her. She said you suggested she ask me about the party."

Gail placed her purse on the counter as she shrugged off her jacket. "Kathy called yesterday asking if I'd talk to her. She set it up so Abby would be home alone after school. She didn't tell Jim, so I didn't think I should tell you until after I'd seen Abby."

"The girl sounded fine on the phone. It must have gone well."

"Not really. Although it did put the party in a new light. What did you tell her about it?"

"Just that I was making plans and would soon be in touch. She asked if she could bring her boyfriend."

"No!" Gail moaned. She slumped onto a stool at the counter. "So that's why she called you. To get back at me."

"What happened between you two?"

Gail told him, then added, "Calling to ask if the boy could come to the party was a direct slap at me."

"He was with her when she made the call," Brad noted. "I heard her tell him it was okay."

"Brad, no! You *didn't* tell her she could bring him!"

"How was I to know what was happening? You never bothered to tell me about Kathy Marshal's call."

"And if I had? Would you have told Abby she couldn't bring the boy?"

"I don't know," he admitted.

"That settles it." Gail stood up. "There will be *no* birthday party for Abby! At least not one given by us." She turned away.

Brad stepped in front of her. "Stop and think, Gail. If we don't go through with the party she'll feel we're rejecting her. That, on top of her alienation with the Marshals, could drive her right into this boy's arms. Besides, you and Kathy may be wrong about Cody. We ought to give him a chance. Give *them* a chance."

"Yes, she might continue seeing the boy out of spite. But encouraging them isn't the answer, either."

"Are you prepared to turn your back on her? To

walk out of Abby's life again forever?"

Before Gail could reply, Brad added, "Well, I can't. I feel as close to her as if she was my own daughter. I won't desert her!"

"Are you insinuating I deserted Abby when I gave her up for adoption?"

"You said it. Not me."

She couldn't believe he'd say or believe such a thing. She had expected him to deny the accusation. At that moment she knew. She couldn't go on like this. The pressures were too intense. On top of her daughter's rejection, Brad's constant interference was more than she could handle.

With hands on hips she glared at him. She spoke then in a low, controlled voice. "Brad, I'm through arguing. I'm through with it all."

"What does that mean?"

"It means I can't live like this any longer. I was on the verge of changing my mind about the party. But this thing with Cody paints a different picture. If you go ahead now, you'll have to do it without me being there. Without me being *here*."

Her mind was racing ahead. She'd put in for more hours at work. She'd look for an apartment close to her mother and Tom so they could help take care of the boys. She would—she would leave Brad.

He was smiling, which infuriated her even more. "Come on, Gail! You're just upset. You're saying things you don't mean. This will look different in the morning. Wait until I tell you my plans for the party."

"Brad. You aren't paying attention. I'm leaving. I'm taking the boys and I'm leaving."

# 12

## *Haunted Hurts*

Bewilderment bathed his face. "Honey, I—"

"I can't talk about it anymore, Brad. I can't keep going over and over the same territory time after time."

She went to their bedroom with Brad following and reached into the closet yanking her overnight case from the top shelf. "I'll pick Grant and Jimmy up at Jen's, then go to Mom's for the night. Tomorrow I'll find a place for myself and the boys."

"You'll what? You can't do that!"

"Oh? I can't? Just watch!"

"You'd leave over a silly thing like this? Turn your back on our marriage because of a party?"

"It's not the party, Brad. Or Abby. It's the things you've been doing in connection with them."

"I've only tried to help you."

Gail's abrupt laugh came out raw, salted with sarcasm. She turned from her packing to glare at him.

"One day you're up. The fun loving Brad I married. The next day you're down. Brooding, angry, someone I don't even know. For awhile I thought maybe you'd found someone else. Another woman."

"I haven't looked at another woman in that way since we got married." His voice had turned low and subdued.

"Which leaves me without a clue as to what's going on with you. I might have taken steps to protect my marriage if there had been another woman. Instead I've ended up shadow-boxing an invisible enemy. I just can't take it anymore, Brad."

His chin quivered, taking Gail off guard. Brad never broke down. It frightened her even more than his anger.

He stood there rigid, arms at his side. "All right. I'll tell you. You couldn't hate me anymore than you do already."

"I don't hate you, Brad. I've never hated you."

"You're telling me our marriage is over," he said grimly. "I've tried my best to distance myself from what happened before we met. Then you started going on and on about your daughter and her fifteenth birthday. It was as though you were taunting me. Like you knew."

"Knew what? I don't know what you're talking about." And, she decided warily, she wasn't at all sure she wanted to know.

He stepped back and leaned against the door, drawing in a deep agonizing breath before he looked at her again. "Gail, the year after you gave birth to Abby, my girlfriend and I aborted ours."

Gail stared at him. "Yours? Your baby?"

He nodded. "I was seventeen. The same age as Abby's father when you found you were pregnant. The

127

girl I was dating was a year younger. We were both from Christian homes. Both active in our church youth group. But we were human, too. We got carried away and she ended up pregnant."

Gail sat down on the bed, her legs weak.

"We were scared. Scared someone would find out. So we decided on an abortion. I drove her to the clinic the day we—" He glanced toward the ceiling, avoiding Gail's eyes.

At last he looked at her again. "Do you understand now? Do you see why your daughter has come to mean so much to me?"

Gail shook her head. "I understand a lot of things. But what has Abby got to do with what happened to you?"

"Abby is the child—I mean, she's come to represent the child I helped dispose of. When you first confided about your pregnancy, I told you we'd never talk about your baby again. I couldn't tell you what I'd done. Not after all you'd gone through to protect your child. I was ashamed. I didn't think you'd want anything to do with me if you found out. I told myself I wouldn't think about it. I'd just lock that part of my life away.

"Then I found Abby for you after realizing how much you needed reassurance she was all right. While I couldn't do anything about the baby I'd helped destroy, I *could* do something about the one you'd given up. I located the Marshals and suddenly it seemed as though I'd found my own daughter."

Gail stood to put her arms around him. "Brad, I'm so sorry."

He was shaking his head from side to side in agony. "I've asked God's forgiveness. But it's still right here." He struck his chest with a fist. "You carried your baby to term while I ran for the nearest exit. No one found out what we'd done. Not our families. Not our friends. No one! But we knew. I knew. God knew."

"Brad, while you may have asked God's forgiveness, it doesn't sound as though you've claimed it. You need to forgive yourself."

She shook him gently. "Honey, you don't have to carry this alone any more. You've finally brought it out in the open. I'll help you."

Later, as they ate the stew Gail had prepared that morning before driving to see Abby, she and Brad continued to talk. He explained his aborted baby was the reason he'd volunteered to work at the primary church camp where they met. It was his way, he said, of making up for what he had done. He related, too, how close he came to halting their developing relationship after she told him about the child she had given up.

"I didn't think I could handle it, knowing you'd gone through what I hadn't been willing to chance. But by then I was more than a little interested in you." He smiled at her. "I think I loved you the moment I saw you get off that old battered yellow church bus with those scruffy little kids clustered around you."

Gail was exhausted by the time she brought the boys home from Jenny's and had them settled in bed. It had been a hard day. Tired as she was, though, she couldn't fall asleep. She lay beside Brad with her arm around him. At last his regular breathing told her he slept.

She'd stand by him, she resolved. She'd help him recover from his grief. Yes, she decided, that was what it was. Grief as well as guilt.

Her mind went then to Abby and the events of that

afternoon. After Brad's confession she was doubly thankful for Abby's existence. If only she could make that clear to the girl.

Gail then made a decision. She made it for Abby, for Brad, and for herself. They'd go ahead with the party. She'd talk to Jim and Kathy and explain why it was so important to Brad.

When the alarm went off, Gail found him lying awake beside her, staring at the ceiling. "I'm not going to the office this morning," he told her. "You don't have to go to work until after lunch. Let's spend the morning together."

"Sounds good to me. Should I call the office for you? Tell them you'll be in late?"

"I'll do it while you get the boys ready for school. I need to tell them what I'd planned for today's issue. Then how about going out for breakfast? Just the two of us."

She kissed him on the cheek. "You've got a date!"

Gail woke the boys, then stopped in the living room for a few moments with her Bible. She usually took time for her daily devotions after everyone had left the house. But this morning  she needed a quick jump-start.

She turned to the book of Isaiah, her eyes lingering on the words King Hezekiah uttered after recovering from illness. Grabbing a pen, she quickly paraphrased the verse on a notepad so she could reread it later.

Brad came into the kitchen just before the boys left the house. Gail glanced at him as Jimmy announced, "Hey, Dad's still home!"

"Good morning," he greeted, making a stab at sounding cheerful.

"Are you sick?" Grant asked. "You always leave before us."

"Just tired. Thought I'd go to work a little late today."

Grant looked at his mother. Was that suspicion in his eyes? she wondered. "Your dad and I thought it might be nice for the two of us to spend some time together before we both have to go to work today. Now don't forget, this is the day you ride the bus home with Kim."

Grant and Jimmy nodded in unison.

"I'll pick you up as soon as I get off work."

"We know," Grant replied.

The sound of the bus lumbering up the street sent the boys racing out the door. Gail and Brad stood in the doorway together, watching the long yellow creature swallow their sons.

Gail reached up to cradle her husband's face in her hands. She stretched to kiss him lightly on the lips. "Are you okay?"

"I don't know. I feel sort of—*numbed* is the word, I guess. How about you? Are you disappointed in me?"

"I'm hurt you didn't feel you could tell me, trust me, before. I can't imagine what you must have gone through all these years, keeping it locked inside, telling no one."

"When I began to look for Abby, the two babies, yours and mine, sort of blended into one. If my child had been allowed to live it would be only a year younger than Abby. When we saw her, it was as if I'd found my own child, now nearly grown."

He shook his head. "It was wrong. I know that."

"So that's why you kept calling Abby *our* daughter," Gail remarked thoughtfully.

They continued to talk over a leisurely breakfast at a restaurant downtown. Once the dam gates opened the flood of Brad's emotion flowed freely. Gail listened quietly as Brad told more about the abortion and his feelings surrounding the loss of his child.

"What happened between you and your girlfriend afterward?"

"We drifted apart. She was hurting, too, although we never mentioned it. Not even to one another."

Gail reached across the table to touch his hand. "There's a poster on the wall at the Crisis Pregnancy Center that states, *Once a parent, always a parent—whether your baby lives or dies*. Of course you've grieved for your child. The problem is, you've never shared that grief with anyone till now. Not even with the baby's mother. You've held it inside until it's nearly destroyed you."

"And our marriage," he added.

"We can put our marriage back together."

"Can we?"

"Yes. We can. We are right now."

Brad was smiling. Already he seemed to be losing some tension. "I love you, you know."

"I know."

From her purse Gail pulled the Bible verse she had jotted down earlier. "You told me you've never felt forgiven. I was reading my Bible earlier this morning when I came across a verse in Isaiah 38. It describes what God does with our sins when we confess them to him. This is my own paraphrase of verse seventeen. 'After suffering sorrow for my sins, God rescued me from the bitterness of my soul, casting my sins from him, placing them behind his back where he refuses to look at them any longer.' "

She touched the back of Brad's hand as it rested on the table between them. "God doesn't taunt us by dangling our sins in front of us after we've set things right with him. You shouldn't either."

He smiled again. "What about you? You've been suffering guilt."

"Yes. That's why I wrote that verse down. I too need to put the past behind me."

Gail found it hard that afternoon to concentrate on work. Yet it helped to force her mind to grapple with the figures flashing across her computer screen. She went through the rest of the day doing the normal things expected of her. All the while questions were building, aching for answers.

That night she found herself watching Brad as he talked to the boys about their day at school. She had been taking his fathering for granted. She appreciated his love for their children. She could well understand his grief in losing his first.

Brad went with her to Grant and Jimmy's room that night to hear their bedtime prayers. He knelt with Gail beside their beds, his arm encircling her.

As Jimmy at last finished a prayer that included the neighbor's cat and her newest litter of kittens, they found Grant watching them with a smile. "Do you guys like each other again?"

Ruffling the boy's dark hair, Brad glanced at Gail. "Yeah. Your mom's a pretty okay lady."

"You've both been mad a lot," observed Jimmy. "Kinda like Grant and me get sometimes."

"It's going to be all right now," Gail assured him.

As they left the room Brad whispered, "I had no idea *both* boys knew something was wrong."

Gail checked a little later to make sure they were asleep. Then she brought a cup of coffee and a bowl of ice cream to Brad in the living room. She sat beside him on the couch, curling her feet under her. "Honey, could we talk some more?"

"Do you still have questions?"

She nodded. "A few. Do you mind?"

"I suppose not. I just hope this doesn't turn into a bone we chew on day after day."

"It won't. It's just that I've been thinking about us. Both of us have been damaged by what we did. Since we can't make it right, we're going to have to learn to live with it."

"That's easier for you," he asserted. "You weren't a Christian when you got pregnant. I was. Yet you chose to give your child the gift of life. I know it's been hard on you, but not nearly as hard as if you had aborted Abby."

"I suppose not." She rested her head against the curve of his arm. "I really don't feel like Abby's mother though, even after seeing and talking to her. I can't figure out exactly what it is I do feel. I care about her. I love her. But it's not the same as I feel for the boys."

She was thoughtful for a moment. "It's sort of like when they handed Jimmy to me in the hospital. I remember holding him, looking down into that little red face, wondering if I could ever love him as much as I loved Grant."

"We'd had Grant longer."

"Yes. I thought of that. When we brought Jimmy home from the hospital I was suddenly busier than I'd ever been in my life, what with a new baby and a toddler. I remember one night getting up with Jimmy while you and Grant were sleeping. I sat watching his tiny face as he nursed. It was then I realized how much I loved him. I loved him every bit as much as his older brother.

"Do you think it might be that way with me and Abby? I mean, I've never had the opportunity to be with her."

"You probably never will either, if you continue feeling it's wrong to involve yourself in her life. You could try being her friend, though."

"I'd like that. But right now she doesn't want even that much from me."

Changing the subject, she asked, "What became of your girlfriend?"

"Last I heard she was married." He looked down at Gail. "I never dated again until I met you."

"I used to wonder if a boy would ever want anything to do with me after he learned I'd had a baby," Gail admitted.

"I dated a couple of guys a time or two after Steve, but I wasn't serious about either of them. If I had been, I'd have told them about my baby. I told you right from the start. I didn't want you to find out later and turn away from me."

Brad took her hand, giving it a squeeze. "I was actually relieved when you told me. At first I was going to tell you about the abortion, but as time went on I couldn't bring myself to.

"Our experiences were so different. I was a Christian. I should have known better. I'd accepted Christ as Savior when I was twelve. But as I grew older I drifted away. I continued going to church. But the Lord didn't seem as important by then."

"I remember how wrapped up in your church you were when we met. That's the one thing that attracted me to you."

"It was guilt that drove me back to God."

"Brad, let's go for counseling. Together. I know I—"

But he was shaking his head. "You're the only person I've ever told. I won't tell anyone else. And I don't want you to, either."

"But, honey, I thought maybe it would help if Jim and Kathy knew—"

"No, Gail. Telling you has been hard enough. I had no choice, since you were about to leave me anyway."

Brad brought the conversation back to Abby and the party. He admitted he had probably made matters worse by telling the girl she could bring Cody.

"I'm having second thoughts about the party," Gail admitted. "Maybe we should go ahead with it. I can't let Abby feel I don't care about her. And as far as Cody's concerned, there's no graceful way to take back our invitation."

"Maybe the boy's not as bad as Jim and Kathy have made him out to be."

"And maybe he is!"

# 13

## When Children Lead

Gail called Kathy the next morning to describe what had happened with Abby the day before. Kathy confessed she had probably been wrong to bring Gail into their problems.

"Abby was angry when I got home," Kathy related. "So was Jim. We had forbidden her to have Cody over when we weren't here. When Jim got home a few minutes before me he wasted no words telling the boy to leave. When I walked in Abby was shouting at Jim. Then she turned on me for 'setting her up' with you."

"It was plain she wasn't happy to find me there," Gail said. "I almost told her I wouldn't see her any more. Then she asked if Brad still meant to give her a party. I made the mistake of admitting I disapproved. She looked so hurt. All this time I thought she wanted nothing to do with me.

"Now I'm wondering if she might have just been testing the waters. She said at least you and Jim and this boy Cody loved her. But Kathy, if she's turning against you two—"

"I see what you mean. She may feel only Cody loves her."

"That's what I'm afraid of."

"Oh, Gail. What are we going to do?"

"Can't you get through to her somehow? Assure her of your love?"

"I've tried every way I know. So has Jim—in his own brusque way. Now I'm scared to death she may not come home from school some day."

"You mean you think she might run away?"

"She wouldn't be the first teenager to run."

"Well—" Gail sighed hopelessly. "I just don't know what to tell you. Or what to think."

"We've got to do *something*," Kathy insisted.

"I think we had better go ahead with the party," Gail suggested at last. "It will give her something to look forward to. It might keep her home and her mind occupied until things simmer down."

"I was thinking the same thing. As much as I've been against it, it just may be what we need."

"Although there's another problem," Gail said, remembering Brad had invited Cody. Kathy groaned when Gail told her. "But that may be for the best, too," Gail said, "If it keeps Cody from pressuring Abby into doing something rash."

Saturday Jenny invited Gail and her family over for lunch. The men and boys went outside while Gail stayed in the kitchen watching Jenny slice vegetables.

Suddenly Jenny demanded, "Okay, Gail. What's going on? We've hardly talked the last few days. I mean really talked, like we usually do."

"We've talked," Gail insisted. "We're talking now."

"You know what I mean. You're tied in more knots than a boy scout could count. What's going on?"

Gail shook her head. "Nothing. At least it's nothing I can talk about. I wish I could."

"Something's happened? Something more than finding your daughter and having this party for her? Is it the boyfriend?"

"Partly."

"I'll drop it. Just tell me it's none of my business."

Smiling, Gail obeyed. "Jen, it's none of your business. I wish I could tell you. But I promised Brad."

"Well, that's an improvement. You and Brad communicating, I mean."

Another improvement came a week later when Beverly and Tom decided to attend church regularly. At the close of a service two weeks later, Gail had watched amazed as her mother and Tom walked to the front, indicating they wanted to become members.

"They can't do that," Gail whispered to Brad. "They can't just up and join the church. They aren't even Christians."

"We don't know that," he whispered back.

Jimmy yanked on Gail's sleeve. "Grandma is *too* a Christian."

Gail bent closer. Cautioning him to keep his voice down, she asked, "How do you know?"

"Cause we was there when she asked Jesus to forget her."

"Forget her?"

Grant leaned across Jimmy. "He means for*give* her."

"Yeah," Jimmy said, "Grant and me told her and Grandpa what to say." Jimmy's freckled face was beaming.

"Oh—" Gail appeared doubtful. "When did this happen?"

139

"The last time we stayed all night with them," Grant whispered again, his dark eyes solemn.

"Let's be quiet," Brad cautioned. "We'll talk later."

Beverly invited them for dinner after church. As Gail helped her mother put food on the table at the apartment, Beverly asked, "Did it surprise you when we went forward?"

"Well, yes. I thought you'd been going to church with us just for the boys' sakes."

The woman smiled. "Remember that Bible storybook I bought so I could have it here to read to them? Well, I started reading it myself. Then Tom got to reading it. Finally he went out and bought us a regular Bible. We've been reading it together ever since."

"Why didn't you say something?" Gail asked. "I could have loaned you one."

"We wanted our own," Beverly emphasized. "One evening while the boys were here we all got to talking about Jesus. Grant asked if we loved Jesus. Tom told him we were just finding out who he was. Jimmy popped up then and told us that wasn't enough. He said we had to *love* Jesus. 'Really love Jesus,' as he put it."

Beverly smiled with the remembering. "They were a persistent duo, I'll say that for them. Tom and I finally told them that was what we wanted to do. Actually, it was more to satisfy them than anything. Grant told us we should pray for Jesus to come into our hearts.

"Tom wanted to know if we hadn't better get down on our knees. That's when Jimmy, bless him, told Tom it would probably be a good idea since we were so old. He figured we must have a whole lot to be sorry for, and God would like it better if we showed him we were truly sorry."

140

Tears came to Beverly's eyes. "I started to pray first. You know—just to make the kids feel good. But I found myself meaning the things I was praying. Then Tom prayed. When we finished, I could tell he felt the same."

Beverly was smiling, her face touched with a new softness. "It was so beautiful. I only wish I had come to this years ago. Things would have been different for you and me. For all of us."

Gail slipped her arms around her mother, holding her close. "I'm happy for you, Mom. For Tom, too. I should have shared my faith with you. I held back, leery of you living so close. Can you forgive me?"

Beverly patted her daughter's cheek. "You have so much more to forgive, honey. I've known how you felt about us moving here, living so close. That's why I had to come. I wanted to reach out to you, to try somehow to make up for the past."

"It seems we're all having problems with the past," Gail said.

* * *

May brought warmer weather, flowers, bees, flies, and yet another litter of kittens at the next door neighbors. It also brought them to the brink of Abby's fifteenth birthday.

There had been no communication between the Marshals and Gail's family except for a note Gail sent Kathy sharing details about the party. In return she received a short two paragraphs back stating they'd be there—with Cody.

Kathy added that they and Abby had reached a stalemate with the three of them treading softly around one another. They were allowing Abby to see Cody at the house once again, as long as one of them was present. Abby was looking forward to her birthday and had cajoled a new dress out of her father for the occasion.

Although Brad was less enthusiastic about the party than he had been, he warmed to it as the day approached, confiding in Gail, "I know it's wrong. But it still seems as though I'm doing this for my own child."

Gail made arrangements for Linda to work for her on Friday, the day of the party. Before Brad left for the office he called Jim. They were still planning to come.

After the boys left for school, Gail drove through a light spring rain to pick up Beverly, taking her to help decorate the small private hotel dining room set aside for their use. On the way she picked up a floral arrangement made of pink rose buds and lavender carnations. Gail and Brad had purchased balloons and paper streamers a few days before. Brad had also run off a long "Happy Fifteenth Birthday, Abby" banner on a computer at the newspaper office.

There were gifts, too. Gail hadn't known what to do about that. She had called Kathy at the last minute for advice. Kathy said that they'd be bringing a gift for Abby.

Gail decided they should probably buy something as well. She found a journal-type diary and added a pen and pencil set. Beverly and Tom purchased a small pocket New Testament. Abby's name was engraved on the cover's rich burgundy leather.

As Friday morning stretched into late afternoon, Gail realized it was time to stop worrying over the consequences. Right or wrong, she could only face into the wind and ride out the storm's crest to—where? To what?

She dressed carefully that evening in a new dusty rose dress with a full gathered skirt. She then helped the boys finish dressing.

"Do we call her Sis, like my friends at school call their sisters?" Jimmy inquired as Gail tucked his shirt into his pants for the third time.

"I think it would be best if you just called her Abby," Gail told him. "While she is your half sister, we'll probably never be close to her the way she is to the Marshals. They're her parents now."

"Cause they adopted-ed her," Grant explained to his little brother. "Didn't they, Mom?"

Gail nodded.

Screwing up his freckled face, Jimmy asked, "Are we 'dopted-ed' too?"

"No, dummy," Grant said. "Mom *kept* us!"

An involuntary shudder coursed through Gail. Searching for words, she told them, "It was different when you two were born. I wasn't married when Abby came along. I wanted her to have a mother *and* a father. That's why I let the Marshals take her."

But their attention had turned by then to shoe tying. Gail turned away, going out to the living room to find Brad dressed in his best gray suit. He was standing at the window looking out on a yard brought to life by the warmer weather.

"The moon will be full tonight," he said, reaching for her as she stepped behind him. He pulled her close. "Are you going to be all right?"

She closed her eyes. Her cheek snuggled against the rough fabric of his jacket. "I think so. Are you?"

"No. But I'll make it somehow. We'll make it together. I've been praying."

"So have I. Pastor Martin told me he'd asked several people to pray for us tonight."

She felt his body tense. "You didn't tell him about me, did you? I mean about—"

"I haven't told anyone," she interrupted. "I do think it would help Jim and Kathy, though, if you let them know why you got carried away into offering Abby this party."

Brad's voice was low but firm. "No! And let that be the end of it!"

The boys were quiet in the backseat on the way to the hotel. It was a beautiful evening. Gail thought of Abby and the Marshals on their way to Linden that very moment. She supposed Abby's boyfriend would be with them.

Beverly and Tom were waiting in the small, brightly decorated room when Gail, Brad, and the boys entered. Beverly wore the aqua lace dress she had worn for her wedding a few months before. Tom presented a distinguished figure in a dark suit and tie.

"We got here way too early," Beverly confessed, fussing with the ribbon atop their gift for Abby. "I was too nervous to stay home once we were dressed and ready."

Slipping an arm around his wife, giving her a quick squeeze, Tom comforted, "It's going to be all right, dear. You'll see."

Jimmy ran to hug his grandparents with Tom catching the boy up in his arms. Grant approached more sedately, looking up at Beverly. "Have you ever seen Abby, Grandma?"

"No. This will be the first time for us all. Except for your mom and dad."

The boy's eyes looked troubled under a furrowed brow. "It feels funny, having a sister I've never seen."

His grandmother bent to hug him, but he twisted

away. "Did you know Mom had a baby before she had us?"

Beverly nodded. "Yes. I knew."

"Did you think it was okay for Mom to have a baby when she wasn't married? Then just give it away?"

Beverly looked toward Gail for help.

It was Brad who came to the rescue. "Your mother was very young. And she was very brave to give her baby up to the Marshals. I want you to remember that. It was hard for her to do. But she did it because it was best for Abby."

"Which one is Abby's mother now?" Jimmy asked. "Our mom or her other mom?"

"Mrs. Marshal is Abby's adoptive mother. Your mom is Abby's birth mother" Brad said. He glanced at Gail. "I thought we'd already answered these questions."

They had left the door open when they entered. A sound came now from the hallway. Gail turned as Jim and Kathy stepped into the room, followed by Abby.

"I'd rather you didn't ask more questions now," she cautioned the boys. "Wait until we're home."

Brad went to greet the Marshals as Gail took note of Abby's white cotton dress with its scooped neckline. A wide red belt cinched the girl's waist, matching her red heels and small red purse hanging from a narrow shoulder strap. She looked much older than fifteen. Especially with her thick dark hair swept up and off to one side.

Abby stole a quick glance at Gail then spoke to Brad. "Thanks for letting me invite Cody."

"Where is he?" Brad inquired.

"Oh, he'll be along," Jim sounded resigned. "That's one thing I'm afraid you can bank on!"

# 14

## Soured Celebration

"Cody's driving his dad's car tonight," Abby responded to Gail while glaring at her father.

"He must be older than you," Gail noted.

"A little. He failed a couple grades."

Jimmy moved to his mother's side, staring at Abby.

"Well," Gail said after an awkward moment, "I guess we'd better start introductions. This is our five-year-old, Jimmy. Jimmy, this is Abby and her mother and father, Reverend and Mrs. Marshal."

Gail looked then at Grant. "That's our oldest son over there. Grant is seven." Gail motioned her mother to come closer. "This is my mother, Beverly Duncan. With her is her husband—my stepfather—Tom Duncan."

Beverly extended a hand to Jim and Kathy before stopping in front of Abby. She held Abby's hand for a time before giving it up. "I've been looking forward to seeing you. I'm your grandmother, Abby. At least I would have been if—"

"Mom!" Gail cautioned. "Please."

"Gosh!" Jimmy commented. "She looks like Grant, don't she?" He rolled his eyes up at his mother. "And kinda like you."

Abby was staring at Grant. "We do look alike."

Kathy, seeming threatened, moved to Abby's side.

"I don't look like no girl!" Grant protested.

"We could sit down, I guess," Gail said, trying to sidetrack a confrontation. She pulled a chair away from the table and turned it around, then reached for another.

Brad and Jim moved to arrange the other chairs in a misshapen circle. Gail overheard Brad apologizing to Jim. "I'm sorry if this is causing a problem for you."

Gail stepped over to where Jim and Brad stood. "When this evening is over I'll fade completely out of your lives again, if that's what you want," Gail told him.

Jim cleared his throat. "We love Abby very much."

"I know you do. And I'm grateful. That was what I wanted for her."

As they joined the others Gail noticed her mother leaning toward Abby as they talked. Abby looked uneasy.

"Brad has ordered steaks for everyone," Gail announced. "I hope that's all right."

"Sounds good to me," said Tom, who had been staying out of the conversation. "Abby, when will your young man be coming?"

"Soon. When you first meet him he may seem sort of—well, different. Until you get to know him."

"That's right," Jim said, "And after you get to know him you realize he *is* different."

"Jim!" Kathy cautioned. "Please."

Abby was watching her father, a smile spreading from her eyes to her lips. "Dad's jealous. I'll always be your little girl, Dad, even when I have my own kids."

Chuckling in spite of himself, Jim returned his daughter's loving gaze. "You've always known how to get around me. Ever since that first day we took you home from the hospital."

"That's the truth," Kathy agreed. "Jim wouldn't leave her alone. One whimper and he was at her side, picking her up, singing to her. I used to remind him 'The Old Rugged Cross' wasn't meant to be a lullaby."

A waitress came to the room then to inquire when they would like to begin their meal. Brad glanced at Abby. "Do you think Cody will be along soon?"

"He should have been here by now."

"We'll wait a little longer," Brad told the waitress.

Twenty minutes passed with still no Cody. At last they decided to start without him. Brad went to find the waitress who promptly brought their salads.

Gail sat across from Abby. A chair at the end of the table, beside Abby, awaited Cody. Kathy chose the chair on the other side of the girl. Beverly placed herself on Gail's side of the table between the two boys. The men at the opposite end were already deep in conversation.

Gail smiled at her daughter. "You look pretty tonight."

Abby's eyes met Gail's for a moment. Then she glanced away. Stiffly she responded, "Thank you." Turning to the door for the hundredth time, her face quickly brightened. "Oh! Cody's here!" she said, nearly upsetting the chair in her rush to greet the young man, who stood out in the hallway looking in.

Jim groaned softly. "You'd think he'd dress up a little for Abby's sake?"

148

"He may have nothing better to wear," Kathy remarked.

"He didn't look *that* bad when he went to church with us."

Gail thought she had prepared herself to meet Abby's boyfriend. She decided now she wasn't prepared after all. Kathy's eyes met her own, reflecting the woman's deep concern.

A chuckle rose from Tom's throat. "A rebel if I ever saw one. Was one myself some years back."

The young couple in the hallway seemed to be arguing. Brad went out to meet the boy, shaking Cody's hand, then bringing them back into the dining room. "Introduce your friend to everyone, Abby," Brad suggested, returning to his place at the table.

The girl's face colored as she stood beside the boy. Gail wondered if Abby's flush was from embarrassment, love, or shame.

"This is—this is Cody Palmer," Abby began. She stumbled over some of their names as she pointed each of them out without mentioning their relationship to her.

It was an arrogant young man who stood before them in soiled jeans, expensive black boots, and dark blue silk-textured shirt open to within inches of his belt. His shirt was topped by a black leather jacket. Strands of brown uncombed hair straggled over his forehead, ears, and collar as he stood with eyes half-closed.

"Sorry I'm late. Was watchin' a ball game on the tube with my old man and forgot the time."

He was good looking in a sullen way, Gail decided. His flat black eyes bothered her more than his clothing. "Won't you sit down?" She gestured toward his place beside Abby. She glanced at Brad. "Why don't you let the waitress know our other guest is here."

Cody slouched onto the chair as a salad was brought and placed in front of him. The waitress looked at him quizzically, glanced at the others, then left without a word.

Abby picked up her fork. She moved a tomato slice from one side of her plate to the other without lifting it to her mouth.

Gail decided Cody must care little for Abby. Why else would he appear dressed like this for her birthday? Gail was sure his lack of taste was not rooted in poverty. Not with such an expensive jacket and boots.

Cody nudged Abby with his elbow as he consumed his salad, glancing sideways at her from time to time. Desperately Gail tried to think of something to say—some way to break the ice now chilling the room.

Before she could find a subject, Jimmy whispered loudly to his grandmother, "Somebody must a' forgot to tell him this was a party. He's still got his play clothes on."

A short masculine chuckle erupted from the opposite end of the table. Abby ducked her head. Kathy shifted uncomfortably.

Cody only grinned. "These *are* my party clothes, kid. Sorry if I'm not dressed to suit your finer sensitivities."

"Huh?" Jimmy stared at Cody.

"You're fine," Gail lied, then added another fib. "We're glad you could be with us tonight."

Cody's shallow gaze met Gail's. "So—you're Abby's real old lady." He glanced at the girl beside him. "Can't understand how you could give somethin' like this up." He slipped an arm around the girl. "Nothin' could ever make me let her get away."

Anger pulsed in Gail's temple. "Sometimes it's best to turn those we love loose for their own good." She felt he caught her meaning as his eyes narrowed.

She was saved from a retort by the waitress, who returned to remove salad plates and refill cups and glasses. Those at the table made a gallant effort to resume their conversation.

As the dinner plates were set before them, steaks still sizzling on heavy metal platters, Gail overheard Cody comment to Abby, "The guy married to your mom must be loaded!"

"She's *not* my mother," Abby shot back under her breath, keeping her eyes diverted from Gail's.

Gail supposed the food was good. But she could choke only bits of it past the lump in her throat. The boy was all wrong for Abby! Gail was sorry about his parents' breakup, which had no doubt hurt him. Maybe he *had* been dealt some raw breaks. But nothing excused his ill manners. *What is this doing to Abby?* Gail wondered.

The murmur of voices mingled with the clink of silver on metal. At last all but Grant and Jimmy had finished. "You don't need to eat any more," Beverly told them, glancing at Gail, who nodded agreement. "That was an awful lot of food for a little stomach."

Jimmy sighed, gratefully putting his fork down.

The waitress removed their plates, then brought in a decorated birthday cake Brad had ordered. She set it in front of the girl as Brad led off singing "Happy Birthday," while Cody sat with an amused half-smile.

Gail and Beverly gave Abby their gifts. Abby seemed pleased. She laughed as Jim handed her theirs. "I've been trying to guess what you had in this box." She opened it to find a pink sweater, squealing in delight.

She was thanking them all when Cody pulled a

small, jewelry-sized box from his pocket. "Here's my gift. I've kept the best till last."

"Cody. That's not nice. I love *all* my presents."

"Just wait till you see what *I* got you."

Slowly she opened the box, then gasped. "It's—it's a ring!" Hastily she snapped the top closed.

Kathy took the box from her daughter and opened it. She showed the contents first to Jim, then Gail.

"A gold wedding band?" Gail questioned.

"It's just a ring, for gosh sakes," Cody protested as Jim sat there glowering at him.

"No, it's *not* just a ring," Kathy flared. "It's a wedding band."

"So?" he shot back.

"My daughter is *not* marrying you!" Jim declared. "And most certainly not at fifteen! I should have stopped her from seeing you long ago."

Cody grinned, lifting a shoulder in a lazy shrug. "You never know now, do you, Rev? Why, one of these days I just might become the father of your grandchildren." He stared at Gail then. "Or I should say *your* grandchildren."

Jim shoved his chair back, rising to his feet as Gail tried to get Abby's attention. The girl appeared to be near tears. "Abby, don't let anything or anyone come between you and your parents. Not me or—" she looked straight at Cody, "or anyone. They love you. They've provided well for you."

"I took it for granted," said Cody, watching Jim warily as the man stood staring down at him, "that you were Abby's father. I nearly forgot how it is with some parents."

He turned his gaze deliberately on Gail then. "That there *are* mothers who desert their kids. Like my old lady did me."

Through the sarcasm Gail detected a cutting hurt. It helped temper the anger she had barely managed to restrain. "I did what I felt best for Abby when she was born," Gail told him. "I don't know all about your family's circumstances. I'm sorry if you've been hurt."

"Hey, lady, I'm fine. Nobody's gonna hurt me like that again. I don't need your pity! I don't need anybody." Smiling then, Cody put his arm around Abby, pulling her against him. "Except you, honey. I *do* need you."

Jim slowly eased himself back onto his chair, hitching it up to the table. "It seems you've done nothing *but* play on our daughter's pity since the day she met you. We all felt sorry for you then. I thought maybe we could help you."

"You mean by spoutin' all that religious propaganda about Jesus?" Cody shot back. "Trying to prove you're better than people like me who don't believe in all that garbage?"

Gail detected Jimmy yanking at his grandmother's arm out of the corner of her eye. Gaining no attention, the boy spoke in a hoarse whisper, "How come Cody don't like us? Or Jesus?"

"Hey, kid, I like you," Cody said with a smile. "I just don't go for all that religious mumbo jumbo. If there ever was a Jesus person he was no better than the rest of us. No better. No worse."

Grant had been listening and watching silently. He now drew himself erect. "Don't you go talkin' about Jesus like that! He's our friend."

Gail turned desperately toward Brad. "Maybe we should go. They'd probably like to clear the table."

But Grant wasn't done. He slipped off his chair to walk around the table while the others watched mesmerized. Grant stopped between Abby and Cody, placing a hand on the back of each chair before speaking to the girl. "Mom says you're my sister."

"I'm your halfsister, really."

"Me and Jimmy must be the only brothers you got."

"I suppose."

"Then since I'm your oldest brother, you oughta know—I don't think Cody's a good boyfriend for you."

"Hey, buddy!" Cody protested. "What business is it of yours, anyway?"

"Abby's my sister!" Grant popped back. His chin jutted out. "You don't like Jesus. But me and Abby and Jimmy and our moms and dads do." Turning to Abby again, Grant asked, "You do, don't you Abby?"

"Yes, of course. But—"

"So," the boy interrupted, "it don't hardly seem right havin' Cody for a boyfriend."

"Grant," Gail coaxed, "That's enough. Cody's right about one thing. This is none of our business. It's between Cody, Abby, and the Marshals."

"But Mom!"

Gail was shaking her head. "Come back and sit down. Right now!"

The others were coming out of their stupor. Kathy got to her feet gathering the gift wrappings and bows. Beverly suggested Tom take Grant and Jimmy to the rest room. Brad went to get the check, while Gail retrieved their coats.

Cody had drawn Abby aside. Gail was relieved when he headed for the door. She stopped, her arms full of coats and jackets, to watch him stride off. She glanced then at Abby, whose face was wet with tears.

Suddenly the girl turned on Jim. "Dad, how could you? Cody's been hurt enough. You're a Christian. A minister. How could you talk to him like that?"

"What kind of father would I be if I saw you headed

for a cliff and did nothing to stop you?"

Kathy moved to Brad's side. "Cody was baiting us. "Can't you see that?"

"I see only that you've hurt him," the girl said, bursting into tears. "I'm going to the rest room."

Kathy started to follow, but Abby stopped her. "Please, Mom, leave me alone for a few minutes."

Nodding, Kathy turned back.

Jim threw up his hands. He looked pleadingly at Kathy and then Gail. "Teenagers! No matter what you do, they make it seem you're at fault. So what now?"

"We love her, Jim," said Kathy. "And pray for her as well as Cody. But mainly we just love her."

"I've failed with that boy."

Kathy managed a strained smile. "Now don't start feeling sorry for yourself. We've enough problems without that."

Brad returned. He placed a hand on Jim's shoulder. "I apologize again. I should have found a way to cancel this party without hurting Abby."

As Gail helped the boys with their jackets, Kathy said, "Grant is so much like Abby at that age."

"I wish we had known her then," Beverly sighed.

Their waitress peered in just then. "Which of you are the birthday girl's parents?"

"We are," said Kathy.

"She just left with that boy. She asked me to tell you."

# 15

## *Three Under the Roof*

"She what?" Jim was halfway out the door when the waitress stopped him.

"It's too late. They're gone."

"I told her she couldn't ride with him tonight!"

The woman shrugged. "I don't know about that. She just gave me the message."

"How could she?" Jim demanded of Kathy. "She's never defied us like this."

Tom moved to Beverly's side, taking her by the arm as he steered her toward the door. He stopped in front of Kathy. "Try not to worry."

Beverly nodded. "I do hope things work out for you. And for Abby."

Tom left Beverly at the door and went back to shake Jim's hand. "We haven't been Christians for long—Gail's mother and me. But I want you to know we'll be praying for you and the girl. For the boy, too."

As they all walked to the dimly lit parking lot, Gail

asked Jim, "Will you call us when Abby gets home?"

"Yes, Gail," Kathy replied for her husband. To Brad she remarked, "Don't blame yourself for any of this. Abby's grown unpredictable since meeting Cody."

Jim came over to the car as Brad was unlocking Gail's door. "I worried at first you meant to force your way into Abby's life. Forgive me for being so abrupt. As you can see, it's hard raising a teenager."

"I'm afraid Abby's inherited some of her mother and grandmother's rebelliousness," Gail told him.

As Brad waited for Tom and Jim to pull out of the parking lot ahead of them, Grant spoke from the back seat. "I did it, didn't I?"

"You did what?" his father asked, watching the boy in the rearview mirror.

"I made everybody get mad."

"Oh, no!" Gail turned toward her son. "I was proud you stuck up for Abby."

Tears flooded his eyes. "She *is* my sister!"

Jimmy huddled by the opposite door. "Why was everyone so mad?"

"Cody wasn't being very nice," Brad explained.

"I don't like him much," announced the boy.

Grant agreed. "He's a real jerk!"

Gail glanced at Brad. "That about sums Cody up. Yet I can't help feeling sorry for him. His behavior may reflect his mother and father's breakup."

"You and Dad almost got broke up, too," Grant said.

She started to protest. "We didn't—" But she had to stop. Grant was right. She had been ready to leave Brad.

Wiping his eyes, Jimmy determined, "I'm going to pray every day Cody will be nicer to Abby."

Gail was beat by the time she and Brad got the

boys home and in bed. Grant and Jimmy's prayers had been long and emotional. Alone at last, she and Brad nearly fell into each other's arms. Gail rested her cheek on Brad's chest as he held her close.

"I hope Jim remembers to call when Abby gets home," he said. "No use going to bed until he does."

It was late, nearly midnight, when Gail finally gave up waiting for the call. "I have to find out what's happened." She reached for the living room phone.

The call did nothing to ease her mind. "We've been here an hour and a half," Jim said, his voice pained. "She's still not home. I could just shake her!"

"Don't do anything to push her away, Jim. Please!" Gail cautioned. "She needs you now more than ever."

"It's that boy. That Cody! This is the first time she's defied us like this."

Once again Jim promised to call as soon as Abby showed up. Gail went to get ready for bed. She needed to be alone. When she returned in her nightgown and robe, she found Brad slumped forward in his chair, praying. He glanced up, holding a hand out to her. She went to him, curling up on the floor at his feet, resting her head on his knee. Together they prayed.

Afterward she checked on the boys, who slept obliviously on. She paged through a magazine then. One o'clock. Two. Still the phone remained silent.

At three, Brad lifted the receiver. The Marshals were still waiting. Jim had called the State Police to see if an accident involving Cody's car had been reported. He then brought up another *what if.* One Brad and Gail had not considered.

"I keep wondering what that boy had in mind when he gave Abby a wedding ring tonight."

After hanging up Brad pleaded with Gail, "Tell me, please, this isn't my fault!"

"Honey, it's not. Really it's not. You didn't know a problem existed when Abby asked to bring Cody."

It was quarter to four when the phone shrilled, breaking the night stillness. Gail jumped, grabbing the receiver as Brad hurried to the kitchen to pick up the other phone.

"Hello?" Gail shouted into the receiver.

For a moment there was only a distant hum on the line, then what sounded like a muffled sob. Gail hung on, waiting until a soft feminine voice inquired, "Is this Mrs. Lorring?"

"Yes! Yes it is. Abby? Is that you?"

"I'm afraid so. Did I wake you?"

Brad's voice boomed in Gail's ear over the line from the kitchen. "Abby! Where are you? Are you all right?"

Silence again.

"That was Brad," Gail explained. "He's on our other phone. We've been waiting for your parents to let us know you got home safe."

A ragged sigh broke from the girl. "I'm sorry about tonight. I—"

Gail detected her repressed sobs. "It's all right, Abby," she comforted. "Don't worry about that now. Are you home?"

"No. I'm at a truck stop cafe somewhere next to the freeway outside of town. Your town. Cody and I drove around after we left the party. It seemed like such a nice night—but then we argued. I got away from him on a country road. There was a sign pointing toward Linden, so I started walking. This was the first place I came to that was open."

"Abby, this is Brad again. What's the name of the truck stop?"

"The Maple Leaf. Just west of Linden. It's kind of scary here in the middle of the night. Since you're closer than my folks, I wondered—I mean, could you come get me?"

"I'll leave right away. Stay inside. I'll come in after you."

Gail heard Brad hang up. "He'll be right there, Abby. I'll have to stay with the boys. But we can talk while you're waiting."

"I don't know what to say to you. I've been kind of awful."

"That doesn't matter now."

"I think, if you don't mind, I'll just hang up and wait for Mr. Lorring. I should call my folks. But I'm kinda scared. I don't know what to say to them."

"I'll call them for you. Why don't you stay with us the rest of the night? We have a spare bedroom."

When Gail dialed the Marshal's number their phone was picked up in the middle of the first ring. "Abby's still in the area," Gail told Jim. "She called us since we live closer. Brad's gone to pick her up. I told Abby she could spend the rest of the night with us. You can drive down tomorrow. Or we could take her home after breakfast since tomorrow—I should say today—is Saturday."

"That's a good idea, Jim," Kathy said on a second phone. "It will give us time to recover so we can better handle the situation when we see her."

"All right," Jim conceded. "But call us back as soon as you find out if she's all right."

Gail prepared the spare room for Abby. Then checked on the boys again. They'd be surprised when they woke to find their half sister in the house. "Lord," Gail prayed aloud as she went to make a pot of hot chocolate, "help us do and say the right things."

She was standing at the kitchen window when Brad

pulled in the driveway. It was a disheveled child, not the maturing young woman they had eaten dinner with, who entered the house. Abby's chestnut hair was tangled. Her red shoes were missing both heels. Her once white dress was soiled.

The girl glanced around the kitchen. She smiled when she saw the mugs of steaming chocolate on the counter. "Mmm. Looks good." For the first time since they met, Abby's eyes met Gail's without hostility. "That's something my mom would do."

Gail nodded. "I have a feeling Kathy and I are alike in a lot of ways."

"Did you talk to my folks? Are they mad?"

"They're worried," Brad told her. "Worried sick, as we all were."

"They were relieved you were all right," Gail said. "Your father agreed you should stay here the rest of the night."

"Thanks. I don't think I could face him right now."

Brad picked up his mug. "I'll leave you two alone and take this to our room. See you in the morning."

"I'll be along in a few minutes," Gail said. She was grateful to be alone with Abby.

"Thanks for coming after me tonight, Mr. Lorring. And for the party. I'm sorry I didn't thank you before running off with Cody."

With Brad gone Gail tried to get Abby to talk about what happened after she and Cody left the party. But Abby had little to say. Finally Gail asked, "Did he rape you?"

"No. But I was afraid he'd try. When he slowed for a stop sign I pushed the door open and ran."

"Are you. . . . Are you pregnant?"

"Just because *you* got pregnant when you were my age doesn't mean *I'm* going to!"

"I'm sorry. It's just that so many girls ruin their lives by getting pregnant. If you feel like I do, abortion is out. But it's not easy giving a baby up for adoption."

Abby turned tired eyes upon Gail. "I can't talk any more tonight. Could I go to bed now?"

Gail led the way to the spare room. "The bathroom's across the hall. I put a clean towel and washcloth on the counter. Is there anything else I can get for you?"

"No thanks. I just want to sleep."

"I put some pajamas on the bed there, and a pair of my jeans and a sweatshirt on the chair for morning. We look to be about the same size."

Gail hesitated before leaving Abby alone. "I'm sorry if I've asked too many personal questions. It's just that after what happened to me, and to the girls I met at the home where I went to wait for your birth, I can't help but be concerned."

Abby turned away as she started to undress. "Please, Mrs. Lorring. I'd just like to go to bed now."

"All right. But could you call me Gail? Mrs. Lorring sounds so—so formal."

"I don't know," the girl muttered, her back turned.

Gail called the Marshals from the kitchen before going to bed. She told them Abby seemed all right, and gave directions for finding the house.

Brad was asleep when Gail slipped into bed. Although she was exhausted, she lay there awake. For the first time, and maybe the last, all three of her children were under the same roof. It was unbelievable. In her wildest dreams she never imagined that would ever happen.

How could she reach the girl? How could she make Abby understand she wanted only to steer her in the right direction? She only wanted to help Abby avoid the trap she herself had walked into so blindly.

It was Jimmy who woke his mother just before ten o'clock. "Dad's getting breakfast. He said you should get up now. Abby's in the kitchen with him."

Gail stretched. She held out a hand to Jimmy, who was still in his pajamas. Jimmy climbed under the covers with her. He nestled down, then twisted his face to look at her.

"We didn't know Abby was here. How come?"

"It's a long story, honey."

He grinned, "I like long stories!"

She smiled at the boy, hugging him tight. "I know you do. But this is one you're not going to hear just yet. Maybe later."

Gail shooed him out of the room and got up, pulling on brown pants and a long-tailed overshirt. She supposed Jim and Kathy would arrive before long. She both dreaded and looked forward to Abby's leaving. If the girl could only accept Gail for what she was—Abby's birth mother who cared enough to place her in a loving environment.

She entered the kitchen to find Abby barefoot, sitting at the counter with a glass of orange juice. She wore the jeans and powder blue sweatshirt Gail had left out. Jimmy was perched on a high stool beside Abby. Grant, fully dressed, was helping his father set the dining room table.

"Good morning," Gail greeted.

Brad turned from the stove after pouring four rounds of pancake batter onto the sputtering griddle. "Hi, I was waiting for you before starting these."

"Thanks." She then asked Abby, "Did you sleep?"

The girl nodded. "Pretty well. Until I woke up and started worrying what Mom and Dad would do to me."

"Maybe you should call them." Gail suggested.

"Mr. Lorring tried. They didn't answer."

"They're probably on their way," Brad said.

Gail nodded. "Most likely. They were terribly concerned about you last night. We all were."

"How come?" Grant asked. "Dad won't tell us."

"You haven't asked *me*," Abby smiled at the boy.

Grant stopped in front of her. "So how come?"

"Cody and I had an argument after we left the restaurant. I was closer to your folks' place than to mine. So I called and your dad came. It was scary out there all alone in the middle of the night."

Jimmy scowled at his mother. "You said the reason Abby was here was a *long* story."

Gail laughed, feeling the tension ease.

After breakfast Grant asked if they could go out to play. Since the morning sun promised a warm day, she said they could as soon as Jimmy dressed. She had hoped she and Brad would have a few minutes alone with Abby before the Marshals arrived.

Abby thanked them again for coming to her rescue as the three lingered at the table.

"I'm glad you felt you could call," Brad told her.

*What can I possibly say to this young woman who just happens to be my daughter?* Gail wondered. *I have to make her understand why I didn't keep her when she was born.*

"I've always cared about you, Abby. From the moment I first learned I was pregnant. I gave you up—"

"I know!" Abby stopped her in mid-sentence. "Because you wanted something better for me. Don't get me wrong, I love my parents. It's just that I can't see how a mother could walk away from her baby. Your showing up caused my folks and me a lot of trouble. We hadn't been getting along anyway."

"Because of Cody?"

"Well—yes."

"I'd think after last night you could see your parents were right to feel as they did," Brad said.

"Yeah. I guess. But when you found us, Mom and Dad and I were arguing all the time. Right in the middle of that, my birth mother shows up.

"I got to wondering if my folks might hand me over to you to get me out of their hair. I didn't know you. But I did know Cody. I decided if it came to that I'd rather go with him than with people I didn't know."

"Your mother and father love you too much to give you up," Gail said. "You know that."

"I do? What am I supposed to think when you keep saying you gave me away because you loved me?"

"Giving you up," Brad countered, "and giving you away aren't the same. Gail let the Marshals have you after protecting you from abortion." He leaned forward. "I didn't have Gail's courage when my girlfriend got pregnant. I was seventeen when we aborted our baby. *My* baby!"

Gail and Abby stared. Gail couldn't believe he was sharing his secret. Briefly he explained, ending with, ". . . and I was a Christian at the time. I knew better."

Abby shook her head. "I don't think I could ever have an abortion.

"That was just how Gail felt," he pointed out.

Abby at last turned to Gail. "Was it hard for you? Carrying me all those months before I was born?"

"It wasn't easy. I was ashamed of what I'd done. I worried about you. I wanted to keep you. I tried to find a way, but none of the options held much hope. For either of us."

Just then the front door burst open and Grant called out, "Abby's Mom and Dad are here!"

# 16

## New Relationships

Grant preceded Jim and Kathy into the house. Brad and Gail rose from the table as Jim approached Abby. Slowly, reluctantly, Abby got to her feet. "Young lady, don't *ever* do a thing like this again!"

"I won't, Dad." Her voice was barely audible. "I'm sorry."

He pulled her into his arms. "We were so worried! So terribly worried!"

"I know—" She clung to him, sobbing.

Kathy watched, her expression grim. "Did Cody hurt you?"

Abby went into Kathy's arms. "No. I didn't give him a chance." She wiped her eyes. "I was so embarrassed when he showed up like that last night. He has other clothes. Then he gave me that ring! He laughed about it later, saying he did it to 'rattle your cage.' "

"Why did you go off with him?" Jim asked

"I don't know. I've been wondering myself."

166

"We forbade you to ride with Cody last night."

A hint of a smile played at the corners of her mouth. "Cody pointed out you said I couldn't ride with him *to* the party. You didn't say a thing about not riding home with him."

Kathy brushed the hair back from the girl's cheek. "Why didn't you call last night, honey? We could have come after you."

"It would have taken too long. The people at the cafe were looking at me kind of funny. A truck driver asked if I needed a ride. The waitress told him to bug off and leave me alone. I was afraid she'd call the police if I hung around much longer."

"I thought maybe it was because you needed your real mother more than us."

"Oh, Mom! No! You're my mother. You always will be."

Abby glanced at Gail. "I'm sorry, Mrs. Lorring. But these are the only parents I've known."

The pain of rejection sliced through Gail. Still she managed a smile. "That's the way it should be."

After stuffing Abby's clothes of the night before in a shopping bag Gail, Brad, and the boys followed the Marshals to Jim's car. Gail wondered if this was to be a final good-bye. Would she ever see Abby again?

The girl spoke to Brad before getting into the backseat. "Thanks again. For everything. Especially for coming after me last night."

She turned then toward Gail. She seemed about to say something. An awkward moment stretched long as they stood at the curb avoiding one another's eyes. Each seemed to be waiting for the other.

At last Kathy cleared her throat. "Gail, I was upset when you found us. Then when you and your husband insisted on giving Abby a birthday party, I grew frightened. But if it weren't for you, we wouldn't have our beautiful daughter."

Kathy took Abby's arm, pushing the girl toward Gail. Her voice rose firm, touched with impatience. "Abby, this is the woman who gave you birth. The one who protected you for nine long months while she was hardly more than a child herself."

The girl twisted slightly, trying to turn away. But Kathy's grip tightened. At last Abby looked up. She glanced at Gail and then back to Kathy. "I know."

"If you could only have seen Gail as we saw her at the hospital. If you could have stood outside the nursery room window with her like we did when she looked at you for the first and last time. Abby, she loved you then and still does. Gail has no intention to try to come between us." Kathy glanced at Gail. "Am I correct?"

A lump swelled in Gail's throat, choking off her voice. She could only nod.

With Abby's arm still locked in her grip, Kathy looked at Jim. "I see no reason our two families can't form a bond of some kind. Work toward a reconciliation of some sort."

The man raised his eyebrows and shoulders at the same time. "I suppose, but—"

"Hear me out, Jim." She turned Abby to face her again, her hands resting on the girl's shoulders. "Honey, you're our only child. You now have two half brothers. But you'll probably never have a sister. Why couldn't we look on Gail as your sister? An older sister. She's nearer your age than your father or me."

During the silence that followed all eyes remained on Abby. Brad stepped closer to his wife. His arm encircling her as a slight tremor coursed through her body.

"I'd like that," Gail offered hesitantly, plugging the silence with hope. "But I'm still willing to stay out of your lives if that's what you want."

Abby slowly raised her eyes to Gail's. "I can't think of you as my mother. I already have a mother and a father." She turned to Kathy and Jim. "I love you guys." Again she looked at Gail. "I'm so mixed up. Shouldn't I feel more for the woman who gave me birth?"

"Relationships take time to develop," Gail offered. "Even when children are born into a family love isn't always automatic. Sometimes it needs space to develop and grow. Would you like having a sister, Abby? Having *me* as your sister?"

Abby didn't reply at once but was almost smiling when she finally spoke. "I guess that would make your boys my nephews."

Jimmy came closer to the girl. He jammed his hands on his hips as he cocked his head to one side. "Does that mean you'd rather be Mom's sister than ours?"

"It might be more fun being your aunt. Sisters and brothers don't always get along when they're young. Aunts like to spoil their nephews."

"We've got a grandma and grandpa who does that!" Grant countered. "Right, Dad?"

Moisture clouded Gail's eyes as she looked first at Kathy, then Jim. "Are you sure about this?"

Kathy's eyes were glistening, too. "I've wished so many times we could have taken you as well as your baby into our home. We knew of your situation—your mother's drinking and neglect, and the foster homes."

Jim smiled at last. "Is this going to turn me into an instant grandfather?"

"Boy!" Jimmy squealed. "We're really gonna have

lots of grandpas and grandmas now."

Abby rolled the car window down as the Marshals drove away, calling out, "Bye—thanks for everything. And Gail—see yah."

Gail caught her breath as she waved. Abby had at last called her something other than Mrs. Lorring. That in itself was a breakthrough.

Brad linked his arm in hers on the way to the house. The boys sprinted to the backyard where their toy trucks waited under the bright, midmorning May sun. Somewhere down the block a lawnmower groaned.

Gail drew in a long deep breath savoring the sweet scents of new growth. "Well, we made it. Made it through fall and winter to spring at last."

She smiled up at Brad as they reached the front porch. Pulling him down to sit with her on the top step, she added, "I wasn't sure we were going to for awhile."

"Abby didn't exactly fall into your arms, but she seems to be coming around."

"I hope so. Maybe taking the emphasis off being her birth mother will help. Bless Kathy for suggesting we try a different approach. And Jim, who didn't insist we end all contact."

"God has been with us this morning," Brad said.

"Yes, I could feel his presence." She gave Brad's arm a quick squeeze. "It's good knowing God cares. I believe if it's in his plan Abby and I will grow close in a special kind of way. God knows I meant to release her when she was born."

"I just wish I hadn't interfered."

"Honey, I don't blame you. Neither should you. At the start you were only trying to help by bringing Abby and me together, even though your reasons did jump the track. At least it forced you to talk about the abortion you had been hiding. Now you can begin your own healing process.

"I had no idea what was bothering you for so long, although I knew something was wrong. I guess I was too wrapped up in myself. In my own torments."

She was quiet for a time, then brightened. "Hey! I've got an idea!"

"Uh-oh. I get a nervous twitch whenever you get ideas."

"I haven't mentioned it lately, but I'm still volunteering at the Crisis Pregnancy Center."

He nodded. "I figured."

"I was just thinking what a team Abby, the Marshals, and I would make."

"A team?"

"At the Center. Mrs. Philips sends speakers out every now and then. They go to churches, schools, places like that." Gail stopped as she felt Brad's body tense. She pulled back to see his face. "Hear me out, honey. Okay?"

"Go ahead."

"Take me for instance. I gave Abby up for adoption. Kathy and Jim adopted her. And then there's Abby, the adoptee." She was watching him. "Don't you see? We could show people how adoption has worked for all of us."

"Kids need to be encouraged *not* to become involved sexually. *Not* to get pregnant, rather than just being taught how to handle it afterward," Brad ventured.

"Well, of course. I should be able to get that across by being honest about my experiences."

"You may have a good idea. But you've left someone out."

"My mother?"

"Me."

Gail bit at her lower lip. "I've gotten carried away again. I'm sorry. I forgot how you feel about the Center."

Brad was shaking his head. "That's not it. I meant maybe I could be part of your team."

"I don't understand."

"It's time I stopped running from my past. If I shared what happened to me, told what I did, what I felt and went through afterward. . . . Well, it might help me come to grips with things. And it might help someone else. I'd be able to give the male point of view, emphasizing why guys shouldn't play around with sex."

She hugged him quick and tight. "Your story would probably do more good than either mine or the Marshals'. But would you dare? With your position on the paper and all?"

"They might listen because of who I am."

Together they sat on the step in the warm sun. "The hardest one to tell was you," he said at last.

She nodded. "I know."

"Telling Abby this morning wasn't so bad, though."

"But to talk about it at an open meeting? Could you handle that?"

"I don't know." Brad released her. He stared out at the street as a tan pickup passed by. "I think I'll have a talk with Pastor Martin." He grinned. "I know, that's what you've been trying to get me to do."

"Mrs. Philips holds counseling sessions at the Center for women still agonizing over past abortions. You might talk to her. In fact, it would probably help her to get the male side of abortion."

A rattle came from the side of the house. "Hey, Dad!

Mom!" Grant called, "Look what we did."

They had hooked the trucks together like a train. But as they negotiated the sharp corner, the lead truck came off. "Nuts!" Grant glared at their creation.

Dejectedly the boys sat on the step below their parents. Jimmy gave a long sigh. "I'm hungry."

"You usually are," Gail noted.

"Will we ever see Abby again?" Grant questioned. "She's kinda okay. For a girl sister anyway."

"I like her better as an aunt," Jimmy said. "Do aunts give kids presents like grandmas and grandpas do?"

Brad shook his head. "I've got to convince your grandmother to stop buying you things all the time."

Grant, who had been watching a ladybug crawl on his hand, looked up at his mother. "Is everything okay with you and Dad now? I mean, can Jimmy and me stop wondering if you're going to get divorced, and if we're going to have to decide who to live with?"

Brad nodded. "You sure can, buddy. I'm sorry if we've made you feel bad."

"Oh, I didn't feel bad. Well, not *too* bad. I prayed about it and I think God heard. I was wondering if I could stop praying so hard for you and Mom now."

Gail slipped down beside her oldest, hugging him close. "I'd like you to always pray for us. We need to pray for one another. Don't you think?"

Squirming away, Grant said, "I guess. But maybe not so hard now. After all, there's a whole bunch of other stuff that needs prayin' about."

"Yeah," agreed Jimmy. "Like who's gonna get me something to eat!"

## *The Author*

Shirlee Evans began free-lancing while her sons were young. Later she went into newspaper writing. She was granted a Washington state Sigma Delta Chi journalism award for investigative reporting.

Her first book, *Robin and the Lovable Bronc,* was published by Moody Press in 1974. After Shirlee left newspaper work, Herald Press published a children's series about the Oregon coastal Indians of the 1800's, which included *Tree Tall and the Whiteskins* (1985), *Tree Tall and the Horse Race* (1986), *Tree Tall to the Rescue* (1987). Other Herald Press offerings included *A Life in Her Hands* (1987) and *Winds of Promise* (1990).

In 1988 *A Life in Her Hands* (a fictionalized account of fifteen year old Gail, who is pregnant) received an Award of Merit from Religion in Media; was named Book of the Year by Choice Books; "one of the most outstanding books of the year" by the University of

Iowa's books for Young Adults program; and accepted for publication in England and Sweden.

This book, *A Life Apart,* catches up with Gail fifteen year later, when the baby Gail bore turns fifteen. The book was written after Karen Evans, and other readers, continued to ask and speculate what might have happened to Gail and her baby after the events recounted in *A Life in Her Hands.*

Shirlee was born in the state of Washington. She and her husband Bob live between Battle Ground and Vancouver, Wash. Their two sons Rod and Dan, and their daughers-in-law Peggy and Karen, have extended the Evans family to twelve with the addition of six grandchildren.

Shirlee is a member of Brush Prairie Conservative Baptist Church.